Katy's Champion Pony

Victoria Eveleigh

Illustrated by Chris Eveleigh

Orion
Children's Books

First published in Great Britain under
the title *Katy's Exmoor Adventures* in 2003
by Tortoise Publishing
This edition first published in 2012
by Orion Children's Books
a division of the Orion Publishing Group Ltd
Orion House
5 Upper St Martin's Lane
London WC2H 9EA
An Hachette Livre UK Company

3 5 7 9 10 8 6 4

The Orion Publishing Group's policy is to use papers
that are natural, renewable and recyclable products and
made from wood grown in sustainable forests. The logging
and manufacturing processes are expected to conform
to the environmental regulations of the country of origin.

A catalogue record for this book is
available from the British Library.

ISBN 978 1 4440 0542 4

www.orionbooks.co.uk

JF

For Anne, my mum, with love and many thanks.

Exmoor

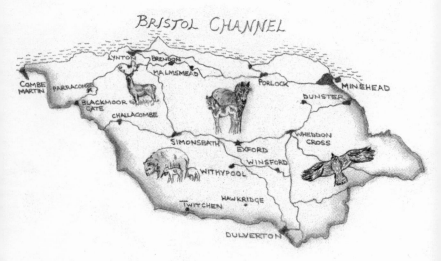

Contents

1

Times Gone By

It was a typical winter's evening – chilly but not really cold, and drizzly but not really raining. Katy Squires and her best friend, Alice, stood in the old cow shed which had been converted into stables for Katy's two ponies at her home, Barton Farm. The girls leaned on the wall inside the shed and chatted as they watched the ponies eat their hay.

Jacko was a liver chestnut gelding. He was fourteen hands high, ten years old and lovely to ride. Somehow he was cheeky and fun but at the same time kind and dependable. Katy had loved him from the first time she'd ridden him at Stonyford Riding Stables. Her Granfer had bought him for her as a surprise birthday present.

Trifle was a registered Exmoor filly who'd been born on the moor above Barton Farm on Katy's birthday nearly three years ago. Katy had secretly bought her from Brendon pony sale. It was hard to imagine that the sturdy, confident pony munching away without a care in the world had, not so long ago, been a timid wild foal. Katy had brought Trifle back to where she belonged, and the little pony seemed to know it.

Jacko and Trifle had been at Barton for nearly two years now, and Katy couldn't imagine life without them. She looked at the contented ponies, breathed in the wonderful stable smell and felt pure happiness envelop her like a warm blanket.

"Look how fluffy Trifle's winter coat is," Katy said. "She looks like a life-sized cuddly toy, doesn't she?"

Trifle realised she'd become the centre of attention. She stopped eating, came to Katy and nuzzled her jacket affectionately.

Alice laughed. "Do you remember Mum winning that huge teddy in the raffle at the New Year's Eve party last year? Be careful, Trifle, or Katy will give you away as a raffle prize tonight."

2

Katy put her hands over Trifle's furry e[ars] "[Don't] listen to silly old Auntie Alice," she said. "F[or a start,] you'd never get up all those steps in the T[ower] would you?"

"Oh well, Trifle," Alice said. "You'll just have to stay here and have a stable sleepover with Jacko." She turned to Katy. "Have you made any New Year's resolutions yet?"

"Mmm. I suppose I ought to," Katy replied. "I wish I didn't like chocolate so much and I want to win lots of rosettes. Oh yes, and I'd love Trifle to become a champion Exmoor pony, of course."

"Are those wishes or resolutions? A resolution is something you're going to do, not something you wish would happen."

Katy gave her friend a light punch on the arm. "Oh, you're such a know-it-all, Alice Gardner! They're a bit of both, I suppose. So what are your resolutions, clever-clogs?"

"Okay. My resolution is to try to be nice to my terrible twin brothers, and my wish is that I'll be happy when we move to new schools next year after the summer holidays."

"I shouldn't worry about that, Alice. We'll all be going together, so at least we'll know some people already. You always seem to get on with everybody, anyway, so you'll be all right."

3

"Um... there's something I've been meaning to tell you, Katy."

Katy was unconcerned. "Well, tell me quickly because we'd better go and get ready for the party."

"I'm going to a different school. A boarding school miles away."

"Oh, Alice! How awful for you!"

"No, you don't understand. I *want* to go."

"But I thought we were best friends," Katy mumbled.

"Of course we are, and we can stay best friends too. We'll still see each other in the holidays, and we can text each other and things, can't we?"

"No we can't! I haven't got a mobile phone, have I? There's no signal here at the farm, remember?" Katy said, angry now. Alice *knew* she didn't have a mobile phone! Not having one made her feel left out at school, but her parents said it would be a waste of money.

"Sorry, I forgot. Okay, we can email each other. Chat on Facebook. I mean, there's lots of ways of keeping in touch."

"It won't be the same, though, will it? Can't you just say you've changed your mind and you don't want to go?"

"Are you crazy? Think what my parents would say!" Alice exclaimed. "Besides, I really do want to go

4

there. I've been for an interview and everything, and it's *such* a cool place. They do loads of games, and they've got amazing stables, with an indoor school and a cross-country course. And there's a big forest nearby with lots of sandy tracks for riding. You can even take your own pony and keep it at livery. It costs extra, but Dad says he doesn't mind paying for me to take Shannon. Isn't that great? His new house is quite near the school, too, and I'll be able to go there for weekends. I've hardly seen him since he split up with Mum, and I do miss him a lot. So I'm really excited about it, actually. I wish you could come too though. You with Jacko and me with Shannon – just think what fun we'd have!"

Alice's tactless enthusiasm cut into Katy. Before she could stop herself she blurted out, "Well, thanks for rubbing it in."

Alice looked bewildered. "Rubbing what in?"

"You *know* that my mum and dad would never be able to afford a boarding school. They're not rich like your family!" Tears started to run down Katy's cheeks. She turned and ran out of the shed.

"Katy! Come back. I didn't mean it like that," Alice called after her.

"I don't want to talk about it!" Katy shouted into the damp night. She was vaguely aware she was being unfair but she was too upset to care, and it

5

was much easier to get angry about things like mobile phones and money than talk about her true feelings. For the past year or so she and Alice had been inseparable friends, both at school and in the holidays. The thought of being parted for weeks – months even – was dreadful, but Alice obviously didn't feel the same way. Why couldn't she see how much that hurt?

The New Year's Eve party was in the local Town Hall. There was a barn dance for all ages, with a band and a caller who told everybody what they should be doing. Some people knew the steps already and others got in terrible muddles, but it didn't matter. The main idea was that everyone got together and had a good time.

To begin with Katy tried to avoid Alice, but it became impossible – especially when Mum and Dad went off to sit at a table with Alice's mum, Melanie.

It was Alice who broke the ice. She came up and said, "I'm sorry, Katy. I didn't mean to. I mean I don't want you to think … oh – you know what I mean!"

Katy still felt betrayed. She wanted to say, *Yes, I know what you mean: you'd rather go miles away to a posh boarding school than stay here and go to the local school with me. I thought we were best friends, but you've ruined everything!* Instead, she said, "Yeah, well, it's okay. Let's just forget about it, shall we?"

Alice gave her a quick hug. "I knew you'd understand!" she said. "Friends for ever?"

"Friends for ever," Katy replied, trying her best to smile.

Alice grabbed her hand and headed towards their parents, who were beckoning to them. "Come on! They need us to make up numbers for the next dance."

It was hard to be unhappy with all the music, dancing and laughter.

Next autumn is ages away, Katy thought. Too far away to worry about now.

They stayed on the dance floor for several more dances until the caller announced, "Take your partners for The West Country Waltz!"

"Let's sit this one out. It sounds complicated, and I'm done in," Katy said to Alice.

They went back to the table where Katy's Gran and Granfer were sitting.

Alice collapsed onto a chair in a mock faint. "We're shattered!" she announced.

"Pah!" Granfer scoffed. "Young people don't have any stamina nowadays. Come on Peggy, love. We'd better show them how it's done." He took Gran's hand and led her onto the dance floor.

"How embarrassing!" Katy whispered to Alice, but her embarrassment soon turned into amazement.

Gran and Granfer danced gracefully and in perfect harmony, their feet hardly touching the floor. People stood and watched in awe as the couple swept round the room with breathtaking style.

"I had no idea Granfer could dance like that, and how does Gran manage with her arthritis?" Katy asked her father.

"When Gran gets her dancing shoes on, nothing stops her," Dad answered. "Gran and Granfer used to win all sorts of prizes for their dancing when they were younger. The money they won helped them to turn Barton into one of the best farms on Exmoor."

For the first time, Katy imagined her grandparents as a handsome young couple with their whole lives in front of them, long before they were Gran and Granfer, or even Mum and Dad.

When the music stopped everybody burst into applause.

Soon it was midnight, and everyone was hugging and kissing and saying, "Happy New Year!" Then they formed a huge circle, held hands with crossed arms and sang *Auld Lang Syne*.

Katy was sandwiched between Alice and Granfer, diving in and out of the circle in a long, snake-like chain as they sang the chorus.

"What on earth does Auld Lang Syne mean?" Katy asked Granfer afterwards.

"Roughly translated, it means times gone by, I think," Granfer explained. "It's Scottish, but over the years it seems to have become a traditional New Year's Eve song all over the place, probably because it tells about how time goes on but friendships should be remembered." He paused, and sighed deeply. "Yes, whatever happens, friends and family should never be forgotten."

A forlorn expression came over him, and for a dreadful moment Katy thought he might cry. Perhaps he'd overheard her row with Alice. She accidentally caught Alice's eye and looked away quickly.

Luckily, Melanie appeared with a tray of drinks. "The glasses with stems are champagne and the tumblers are lemonade," she said.

Granfer handed Katy and Alice tumblers, and took a couple of glasses of champagne for Gran and himself. "Thanks, Melanie," he said. He raised his glass and smiled. "To times gone by!"

"To times gone by!" the girls repeated. Katy took a sip of lemonade and the bubbles went up her nose.

The Squires family got home from the party in the early hours of the morning. Gran and Granfer stayed at Barton Farm for the night so they didn't have to drive back to their bungalow.

Mum had just finished cooking breakfast the following morning when the telephone rang.

Dad sat at the kitchen table, eating his eggs and bacon. "Who on earth could be ringing at this time of day?" he grumbled. "My New Year's resolution is to ignore the phone at meal times."

Mum gestured to him to be quiet. "Barton Farm. Can I help you? Oh! Hello, Rachel. Happy New Year to you too. What? Well, that's marvellous news! Congratulations! I'm thrilled for you both. Jack and Peggy are here, so do you want a quick word? We'll see you soon. Okay. Love and congratulations to Mark. Bye, now." She handed the phone to Granfer.

"Hello, Rachel love. Well done. I expect you want to speak to Mum, then. Yes, you too. Take care, now," Granfer said.

Gran took the handset from Granfer. "Hello? Congratulations, darling! I'm so pleased. What?

10

Yes, of course Dad's pleased too. He's just, you know, it takes a bit of time… Yes, I know. Oh, how lovely…"

"What's going on?" Katy whispered.

"Auntie Rachel and Mark are engaged," Mum whispered back.

"Wow! They're getting married?" Katy exclaimed.

"Ssshhhh!" Mum and Dad hissed together.

"There's too much noise in here, Rachel. I'll just go into the hall," Gran said, giving the family one of her stern looks.

With Gran talking in the hall, everyone talked more normally in the kitchen, although they were secretly trying to eavesdrop on Gran's conversation at the same time.

"You were a bit short on the phone, Jack," Mum said to Granfer.

"Oh, you know me. I hate talking on that contraption," Granfer said. "I'm very happy for them both. Delighted. Over the moon."

Katy sensed Granfer wasn't nearly as happy as he made out. She knew how fond he was of his only daughter, and guessed it was hard for him to let go, even though Mark and Rachel had been going out for ages and everyone had assumed they'd get married one day. The idea took some getting used to, she had to admit. For a start, it was bound to mean Rachel

11

would spend less time at Barton Farm. Since Katy had become the proud owner of Trifle and Jacko she'd grown to rely on her aunt's visits. Looking after two ponies was an awesome responsibility, and Rachel seemed to have all the answers to Katy's frequent questions.

"You're what? You can't be! When? That soon? Oh dear! Yes, of course it's a great opportunity, but…" Gran's voice became alarmed.

They all fell silent, straining to hear what she was saying.

A few minutes later she returned to the kitchen, looking flustered. "Oh dear! I can't believe it!"

Dad leaped up and helped her to her chair. "Can't believe what?" he asked. "That Rachel's getting married at long last?"

"No, of course not! We all expected that! No… Oh dear, I don't know how to tell you this, so I'll just have to come out with it straight. Rachel says Mark's uncle has offered him a job running a huge cattle station in Australia. They're going to live out there just as soon as they're married. They're moving to Australia this summer! Oh dear!"

Granfer got up from his chair and put his arm round Gran's slumped shoulders. "Don't take it so hard, love. It'll be okay. We'll go out and see them, if you like. It's not far nowadays. I've always fancied a trip down under."

Gran looked up at him with watery eyes. "You knew, didn't you? How come you knew?"

Granfer forced a smile, but his face looked sad. "Mark came to see me yesterday to ask for our daughter's hand in marriage. Very proper and correct, as always. He told me then. Said I wasn't to breathe a word to anyone until he'd asked Rachel to marry him."

Now Katy understood why Granfer had looked so sad last night when he'd said friends and family should never be forgotten.

I don't like this year much, Katy thought as she put the ponies out in the field later that morning. What other surprises has it got in store?

She watched as Jacko and Trifle cantered off together.

Alice had promised to be her best friend for ever, and Rachel had promised to help her train Trifle, but they'd either forgotten or didn't care. Both had made different plans for the future, and Katy was no part of them. She remembered raising a glass to times gone by a few hours ago. Time moves on and people move on with it, she thought sadly. What if friendships aren't remembered? What if Alice and Auntie Rachel make new lives for themselves and forget about me? How on earth am I going to cope without them?

2

Horses of a Lifetime

Rachel would be missed by many people when she went to Australia, but she'd also be missed by the horses she cared for. She understood them and they felt safe with her. Katy knew the one who'd miss Rachel most was New Moon. He was a six-year-old thoroughbred, and he had a white marking like a new moon between his eyes. In the middle of the moon there was a perfectly placed large whorl, where hair grew out in all directions from a central point. The rest of him was bay, with a black mane and tail, black legs and a body the colour of a polished conker.

Moon had been sent to Rachel for re-training because he attacked anyone who came within biting distance. However, he instantly seemed to know he could trust her, and soon he was greeting her with pricked ears and a whinny rather than snapping teeth. Unfortunately, on returning to his rough owner he'd slipped back into his old ways. The owner had contacted Rachel to demand his money back, saying the horse was incurably dangerous and was going to be put down, so she'd bought Moon for the same price the abattoir would have paid.

Within a year, Rachel and Moon had won many prizes in local competitions, and Moon had become one of the best hunters on Exmoor. He was beautiful, fast, sure-footed and sensible, and he would do anything for Rachel. Moon was her horse of a lifetime.

Several people had told Katy that Jacko would be her pony of a lifetime, and in many ways they were probably right. He was a perfect pony: well-behaved, kind and always willing, with just enough sparkle to be fun. She adored Jacko, but she knew someone else had spent a lot of time training him to be that good. She wasn't inclined to have favourites, especially where horses and ponies were concerned, but if she *had* to choose one, she felt sure it would be Trifle. Katy had known her from the day she'd first found her, cold and wet, as a newborn foal on the moor, and since then a strong bond had grown between them. They'd both been born and bred on Exmoor, they shared the same birthday and – Katy was aware this sounded a bit fanciful, but she truly believed it – they were destined to be together.

Trifle had been taught everything she'd needed to know about living in a herd and surviving on the moor by her fellow Exmoor ponies, but Katy had taught her how to survive in a human world. At first the little filly had been terrified, but Katy's love and patient handling had gradually tamed her. She knew they had a long way to go before they'd be able to gallop together across the moor, but Katy was in no doubt that it would happen one day. Well, sometimes she wasn't so sure, she had to admit.

For instance, she doubted it for a while one frosty evening in January. She was tired after a day at school and she was missing her favourite television programme, but Rachel had come over especially to help her. Trifle had started being difficult when she was led, so Katy and Trifle were practising what Rachel called "groundwork".

Trifle was supposed to be standing still, but she whinnied loudly for Jacko and barged passed Katy as he answered from his stable, forcing her to jump out of the way to avoid being trampled.

"You're not being firm enough with her, Katy. Don't let her move your feet. *You* must control *her* movements; she mustn't be allowed to control yours. Remember, the boss horse controls other members of the herd by moving them around," Rachel said. "Teaching a horse to stand still is really important. You'll be riding her soon and she'll have to stand still while you mount and dismount for a start. You never know when you might need Trifle to stand as still as a statue, from the line-up at the Horse of the Year Show to something rather less glamorous. It's really useful if a horse stands still on command if you fall off, for example. In fact, there are situations where it could make the difference between life and death. Let's try again, shall we? Make her go back to where you told her to stand in the first place."

"Easier said than done!" Katy mumbled as she pushed into Trifle's shoulder to make her go backwards.

Trifle sidestepped and tried to give her a playful nip.

Without thinking, Katy slapped her on the nose in self-defence.

Trifle shot backwards with her head in the air, nearly pulling Katy off her feet.

"Ow! Stop it!" she yelled, pulling down hard on the rope and glaring into her pony's eyes.

Trifle took fright at this unexpected aggression from a person she usually trusted. She pulled away, hurting Katy's cold hands, and kicked out sideways as she wheeled round. Then she galloped towards the gate, whinnying for Jacko, slipping on the frozen ground and tripping on the trailing rope.

"Well, what have you just learned?" Rachel asked calmly.

"That I'd rather be inside watching television," Katy replied truthfully.

Rachel smiled. Then she caught Trifle and worked with her while Katy watched and listened. There was something in Rachel's quiet, confident manner which made the pony pay attention and concentrate. With the slightest of body movements, Rachel made Trifle go forwards, backwards and in circles.

"I hope you see why I told you to wear gloves and a hard hat," Rachel said as she worked. "Bangs on the head aren't a good idea, and it's difficult to stay calm when all of the skin has been ripped off your hands. Well done for not having the rope wrapped around your hand. I remember your dad being dragged across a field by his pony because he had the rope looped around his hand and couldn't free himself. He was badly hurt but your Granfer still gave him the most awful telling-off. Poor Phil! He really didn't have much luck with ponies." She led Trifle closer. "Now then, do you see what I'm doing here? I'm putting pressure on the head collar by pulling lightly on the rope, but as soon as Trifle responds I let the rope go slack and that's her reward. If you don't give at the exact moment she does the right thing, there's no reward for her and you'll make her confused and unsure of what you want. Then it's a downward spiral because you'll have to use more and more pressure to get a response. Come and have a go yourself."

Trifle did exactly as she was asked. "She just didn't understand what I wanted before, did she? She follows my every move now," Katy said, smiling.

"The same principle will apply when you start riding her. Exmoor ponies are very intelligent and you can make them sulky very easily if you nag them or treat them unfairly." She stroked Trifle's forehead. "We don't want that, do we sweetheart?"

Katy shivered. "Brrr! I'm getting so frozen that my feet are nearly dropping off. Do you mind if we go in now?"

"No, that's fine. I was going to stop, anyway. It's a good idea to keep lessons with young horses short, and always end on a good note. Don't worry when things go wrong. They often do, but the great thing is to put them right, like we did today."

"Like *you* did today, you mean!" Katy replied. "How am I going to ride Trifle without your help?"

"You'll manage. We're doing the important training now. She'll be a doddle," Rachel said confidently.

"May I have that in writing?" Katy asked, sounding much more light-hearted than she felt.

*

On the first day of April it was Katy and Trifle's shared birthday. They celebrated by giving the family a display of the skills they'd learned since the New Year. Alice and Melanie came over to watch as well. Katy had kept Trifle at Stonyford, Melanie's riding stables, for her first winter.

Katy led Trifle around in a circle, walking and trotting. Then she attached long reins to each side of Trifle's head collar, as Rachel had taught her, and drove the pony through a maze of poles. Trifle even backed up for several steps, and trotted over a very small jump. For a grand finale she walked over some black plastic silage-wrap and stood still on a marked spot for at least a minute.

"That's incredible!" Katy overheard Melanie say to Rachel. "I can still remember the scrawny, frightened foal we transported to Stonyford from Brendon sale. The change in that pony is truly amazing. You've done a great job."

"Oh, I just pointed them in the right direction, that's all. It's entirely down to Katy's hard work," Rachel replied. "Those two really seem to have something special going on between them, don't they? Katy's very talented."

Rachel's words were a wonderful birthday present which Katy stored away. She had a feeling she might need to draw strength from them sometime.

When they had finished their display, Katy bowed and everyone clapped.

Trifle had never heard clapping before. She shot backwards in alarm, but Katy managed to hang on to the rope.

"You'll have to get her used to clapping and loud noises before you take her to shows," Granfer said. "You know the saying, don't you?" He continued before anyone could answer. "An amateur practises until he gets it right. A professional practises until he can't get it wrong."

"Well in that case, you'd better start practising being a bridesmaid, Katy. I certainly don't want any amateur bridesmaids at my wedding," Rachel said.

"Wow! You want me to be your bridesmaid?" Katy exclaimed.

"If you can put up with wearing a dress and walking down the aisle with Greg, who's going to be Mark's best man," Rachel replied.

Alice was making embarrassing swooning gestures, but luckily no one else noticed. She knew Katy had a crush on Mark's youngest brother, Greg.

Katy blushed. The thought of walking down the aisle with Greg was like a dream come true. "I think I could put up with that," she said coolly.

3

The Wedding

It was a perfect wedding. The weather was sunny and clear, everything went as planned and, best of all, Greg actually linked arms with Katy to walk down the aisle. Katy walked slowly to make the moment last as long as possible. A carriage pulled by a pair of grey Shire horses took the bride and groom from the church down the hill to the hotel where the reception was held.

The same band which had played at the New Year's party was there, and soon everyone was up and dancing. Greg asked Katy to dance.

As they danced, Greg caught her eye and smiled

his heart-stopping smile. She felt herself blushing, and smiled back. I know he's ten years older than me, she thought, but Dad's nine years older than Mum, so perhaps when I'm older…

Her daydream was interrupted by the caller announcing, "Take your partners for The West Country Waltz!"

"May I have the pleasure of this dance?" It was Granfer.

"How about Gran?" Katy asked.

"She wants to sit down. It's been a long day."

"But I don't know what to do, Granfer. I can't dance properly like you can."

"No such word as can't," Granfer replied, guiding her to the centre of the floor. "Just let me do the steering, okay? When I move, you move with me."

"A bit like training Trifle," Katy giggled.

"Exactly!"

Katy would remember that dance all her life. Granfer literally swept her off her feet. Her long, sky-blue silk bridesmaid's dress swirled around her and she felt very grown up. How fantastic to dance with a person who knew exactly what he was doing, especially when that person was her wonderful Granfer. It was only when the music stopped that Katy realised they'd cleared the floor and everybody was clapping.

"Do you always clear the floor when you dance?" she asked Granfer.

He smiled mischievously. "Only when people are afraid the woman I'm dancing with will tread on their toes!"

Rachel and Mark gave Katy a silver photo frame as a present for being their bridesmaid. There were three windows for pictures. Katy chose her best photos of Trifle and Jacko to put in two of the windows, and one of Rachel on Moon to put in the third.

O n the day before Rachel and Mark left for Australia, they went to Barton Farm for a farewell tea. Afterwards, all the family gathered outside to say goodbye.

Katy stood next to Granfer. He kissed Rachel and said softly, "I'm letting you go only if you promise to come back home if you're unhappy." Then he raised his voice. "Have a safe journey then, Rachel love. Good luck."

He shook Mark's hand. "Take care of her," he said, and then he hurried indoors.

Katy hugged Rachel. "Thanks for all your help, Rachel. I'll miss you so much."

"Not half as much as I'll miss you. Take care of yourself and that cheeky little pony of yours. I've left a present for her outside her stable, by the way. Oh, and

Katy, try to look out for Moon, will you? A man called Mr Jackson bought him. He lives in that house with a lovely garden and a stable block right next to the road just outside Winsford. He's really nice, and I'm sure Moon will be very happy there."

After they'd waved goodbye to Rachel and Mark, Katy's family went back into the house but she couldn't resist finding the present. It looked like a bulky bag of rubbish leaned up against the stable door. There was a note attached to the bin liner. She read Rachel's bold, rounded handwriting:

For Trifle and Katy.
Sorry I can't be here to see these put to good use.
Have fun!
Much love, Rachel
PS Trifle already knows because I had to make sure they were a perfect fit!

Katy tore the thin black plastic, and the smell of new leather wafted out. She peeled away the rest of the bag. A beautiful nut-brown saddle with a matching bridle lay on the floor in front of her.

"Thank you, Rachel! Thank you so much!" she shouted at the car disappearing down the farm track.

4

A Ride to Remember

It was the first week of the summer holidays, and
Melanie was driving Katy and Alice from a Pony
Club rally in her smart new horse lorry. Jacko and
Shannon were travelling in style in the back.

The lorry swayed gently along the winding road.
Katy knew the route well, but everything looked
different now she could see over the hedges from her
seat high up in the cab. She imagined riding over the
countryside spread before her.

Melanie broke the silence. "What are you doing for
the rest of the holidays, Katy?" she asked.

"Nothing much," she replied. "I mean, we're not going away or anything."

"You see, I'm taking Alice and the twins on a riding holiday next week, and I was wondering whether you'd like to come too."

"Oh, please say you'll come!" said Alice. "I need someone to protect me from Josh and Rupert." She found her younger twin brothers very annoying.

"You do talk nonsense sometimes," said her mum. "But it would be lovely if you could join us, Katy. We'll be away for three days and two nights. I've planned a circular route over Exmoor, with places to stay which take horses as well as people, so it'll be quite an adventure."

Katy hesitated. It did sound like fun, but it also seemed pretty daunting. She'd hardly ever stayed away from home, apart from an occasional sleepover party, and there was also the problem of Alice. Somehow things hadn't been the same between them since their argument about schools on New Year's Eve. They were still friends, but there was a wariness to their friendship which hadn't been there before – a conscious effort not to mention new schools or anything about what would happen after the summer holidays. Occasionally the subject had bubbled to the surface and burst into a quarrel. The last time that had happened, Alice had called her chippy, whatever that meant. What if they fell out in the middle of their ride? They'd be stuck with each other, no matter what. But how could she refuse when she'd already said she wasn't doing anything?

"Do say yes!" Alice said. "We'll have a great time, and so will Jacko and Shannon. They'll love it!"

"But what about Trifle?" Katy said. "She'll be terribly lonely without Jacko. She's always had a horsy companion, ever since she was born. She frets terribly when Jacko's away for a day – I have to keep her in the stable because I'm afraid she'll hurt herself dashing around in the field calling for him. She can't be shut in a stable for three days though. It wouldn't be fair on her."

"Well, why doesn't Trifle have a holiday at Stonyford while we're away on our holiday? She could run in the bottom meadow with her old friend, Promise. I'm sure they'd love to see each other again."

Promise and Trifle had shared a field at Stonyford for their first winter, and Trifle had occasionally been used as a companion for Promise since then, especially when travelling. Trifle already had two special talents: she seemed to get on well with every horse or pony she met and she loved travelling in horse boxes or lorries. Melanie said that horses and ponies who had grown up in herds often had good "social skills" and knew how to get on with others, but nobody could understand why

Trifle liked travelling so much. Whatever the reason, it made her a very useful pony.

"Oh, all right then," Katy said, and realised it sounded rather ungrateful. "I mean thanks very much. I'd love to come. And I'm sure Trifle would love a holiday at Stonyford."

"Brilliant!" said Alice, grinning and squeezing Katy's knee. She seemed genuinely delighted.

The rest of the journey was spent discussing equipment, routes and accommodation. By the time they arrived back home, Katy was as excited as Alice.

The following Tuesday, after a big breakfast, Melanie, Alice, Katy, Josh and Rupert set off from Stonyford in blazing sunshine. The rucksacks on their backs and the head collars under their horses' bridles added to the thrilling feeling that they were starting out on a great expedition.

Penny, Melanie's assistant, waved them off. She'd be taking out rides and looking after things while they were away.

As they rode by the bottom meadow, Trifle and Promise hurried over to see what was going on. Then, as if sharing a private joke, they squealed and charged off round the field, tails in the air, thoroughly enjoying themselves.

By the time the riders reached Brendon Common a couple of hours later, black clouds had blotted out the sun. They'd just crossed the river by a deserted village when heavy drops of rain began to fall. Josh and Rupert, who'd wanted to gallop all the way to begin with, now lagged behind and complained bitterly that they were cold, wet, bored, aching and hungry.

Suddenly, as they approached a ruined farmstead, the heavens opened and there was a spectacular thunderstorm. Hailstones like billions of white frozen peas crashed to the ground and covered everything in a slippery layer of ice. They stung the ponies and made them prance around. Josh started to scream. His pony bolted, with Rupert's following hot on his heels. Melanie hurried after them.

Alice and Katy tried to shelter by a broken-down wall.

"Well, they did say they wanted a gallop!" Alice said, smiling mischievously.

"Poor things! I hope they're okay. You are horrible to your brothers, Alice!"

"You would be too if you had to live with them," Alice replied. Then she looked serious. "I'm so glad you've come along. I don't know what I'd do without you."

"Well, you'll find out in September, won't you?" Katy said before she could stop herself.

"Oh, for goodness sake! I was only trying to be nice!" Alice exclaimed.

Katy's fears were coming true. She and Alice were falling out before the holiday had really started. "Sorry. Let's make a pact: no talk about school and no talk about friendship. Okay?"

"Okay," Alice said quickly, because at that moment the others came round the corner. Melanie was leading Josh and Rupert, and both boys were sobbing.

"Miraculously we're all in one piece!" Melanie said with false jollity. She looked very shaken.

Soon the storm blew over, and the bedraggled party made its way over a boggy stretch of moorland. They walked in single file, following Melanie as she picked her way over the treacherous ground. The sun was surprisingly hot when it did come out, and the riders and ponies steamed like boiling kettles.

Eventually they reached a gate which led to a lane. Melanie stopped and handed round some rather squidgy chocolate bars. "This isn't much of a lunch, I'm afraid, but we all had a big breakfast and we'll get a good meal tonight," she said.

She pulled a mobile phone from another pocket. "Hurray, a signal at last. I wonder why anyone has mobiles on Exmoor. You can hardly get a decent signal anywhere." After a long conversation with Penny at Stonyford which featured the word "sorry" a lot, she put the phone back in her pocket and said, "Well, that's settled, boys. Penny's going to pick you and your ponies up after breakfast tomorrow morning and take you home."

The twins looked overjoyed.

"But you must promise me you'll be good. Looking after you two most definitely isn't in Penny's job description, so she's doing us all a great favour."

"You're telling me!" Alice whispered to Katy.

"We promise!" the twins sang out together. They often did things at exactly the same time, as if invisible communication waves passed between them. Katy wondered what it would be like to have a twin sister, or any sister at all come to that. She thought of Auntie Rachel, and felt a sudden pang of loss.

Hooves clacked smartly against the tarmac and everyone was in high spirits again as they trotted down the lane into Exford, where they were booked into a hotel for the night. Their first goal was in sight.

"I can't wait for a cup of tea," Melanie said.

"And a hot bath," said Alice.

"Both!" said Katy.

"Yes, both," Melanie agreed. "But ponies come first, remember."

The accommodation for the ponies was nearly as smart as a hotel. The stable block was a livery yard for the horses of local people and hotel guests and, by coincidence, it was where Rachel had worked before she'd left for Australia. It was set around a courtyard so all the occupants could see one another, and the loose boxes were large and sturdy. Each had a couple of water bucket holders by the door, a cast iron hay rack in the left hand corner and a stone manger in the right, polished by generations of hungry horses licking up the last morsel of food. The worn square-cobbled stable floors were covered with a thick layer of crisp straw which was neatly banked against the walls. There was even hot water in the yard, so the ponies could be given a relaxing warm shower after their long ride.

Jacko grabbed a mouthful of haylage and stood munching it with his head over the stable door, ears pricked and nostrils quivering, eagerly taking in his new surroundings.

"Night, night, my lovely boy. Won't you have a lot to tell Trifle when we get home?" Katy said. Then she followed Melanie, Alice and the twins into the hotel.

Katy had never stayed in a hotel before. She and Alice were sharing a twin-bedded room. Everything was clean – almost unnaturally so. The sheets and duvets were bright white, and on the wall opposite the beds there was a large, shiny TV screen. On a side table near the door there was a kettle, a couple of cups and saucers and lots of packets of coffee, tea, hot chocolate and sugar. There were also several little cartons of long-life milk and some individually wrapped biscuits. The bedroom even had its own bathroom, with gleaming chrome fixtures, fluffy white towels and a basket full of tiny wrapped soaps and bottles of shampoo, shower gel and conditioner.

The room was a bit like a house in miniature, and the girls wasted no time in making themselves at home. They turned on the TV, made hot drinks, ate all the biscuits, lay on the beds and made full use of the exotic-smelling bottles in the bathroom.

That night, after a delicious supper of steak and chips followed by apple crumble and ice cream, they lay in their beds and watched their favourite programmes for ages. This is the life! Katy thought to herself.

The twins left for Stonyford the next morning, and the girls set off with Melanie for day two of their adventure. The extreme weather of the previous day had been replaced by a grey blanket of warm mist. Soon they were on a narrow bridlepath which ran beside a meandering river as it flowed downhill. On either side of them the slopes of the valley were covered in bracken and gnarled trees.

"Don't those trees look like little old men, looming out of the mist like that?" Katy said, shivering. "Have you heard Granfer's tale about the ghost of Tom Faggus?"

"No, and I'm not sure I want to either. I hate ghost stories," Alice replied.

"Well, he was a highwayman, but a nice sort of outlaw – a bit like Robin Hood. He must have been nice because he loved horses, and his favourite horse in the whole world was his faithful mare, Winnie. He used to creep up on people unawares because Winnie wore leather boots on her hooves. Granfer says that whenever it's misty the ghost of Tom Faggus returns to the moors, creeping up behind..."

"Katy! Shut up!" said Alice.

"Sorry, but it really is supposed to be true," Katy said, smiling apologetically.

As they rode down the valley the mist became thinner. After a while, Alice's sharp eyes spotted a dark shape in a clump of bracken. It was a red deer calf. "Oh, it's adorable!" she exclaimed. "Do you think it's been abandoned? Perhaps we should take it with us and find a vet or somebody to take care of it. Will you hold my pony so I can go and stroke it?"

"Um... I don't think that's a good idea," Katy replied. "Granfer told me that a hind will hide her calf in an overgrown place like that while she goes off to graze."

"Isn't a female deer called a doe?" Alice asked.

"I think red deer are different. Dads are stags, mums are hinds and babies are calves, as opposed to roe deer which have bucks, does and fawns. It's all very confusing, isn't it?" Katy said.

The grey silhouette of a hind appeared on the hazy slope above the riders. She hesitated when she saw them and then started to move away, so they moved on quickly in case she was the mother of the calf.

They rode in silence. It was the sort of silence which happens when all the safe topics of conversation like the weather, horses and wildlife seem to have been exhausted and the thing which is on everybody's mind – new schools, for example – can't be mentioned.

"Is everyone okay?" Melanie asked.

"Yes, fine," the girls replied.

Melanie gave a look as if to say she didn't quite believe them, and embarked on a long story about the farm they were riding through.

The story came to an end and the track joined a road. As they trotted along, Jacko's hoof beats sounded rather odd.

"Typical!" Melanie said, sighing. "Jacko's got a loose shoe. That's all we need!"

"But he's only just been shod!" Katy protested. It looked as if the twins wouldn't be the only ones to have their riding holiday cut short.

They were passing a smart-looking house

surrounded by a beautiful garden, with a modern stable block right next to the road. A horse and a small pony were standing in the yard, and a tall, grey-haired gentleman was pushing a wheelbarrow out of a stable.

"That horse looks like Moon!" Katy exclaimed.

The man came over to greet the riders, his hand raised in a welcoming gesture. "Did I hear you say Moon?" he asked.

Katy blushed. "Oh dear, is my voice that loud? My Auntie Rachel sold him to you, didn't she?"

"She did indeed! So you must be Katy. What a pleasure to meet you!"

"I'm really glad to meet you too. I promised that I'd look out for Moon, you see."

"Well, you'd better come on in and give him a thorough inspection then. Goodness me, I'm forgetting my manners! The name's Jackson. John Jackson," he said, reaching up to shake Melanie's hand. "Why don't you all tie up your horses and come in for a cup of coffee or whatever, eh?"

Melanie shook his hand. "That's very kind of you, but I think we'd better press on. Katy's pony has a loose shoe, so we've got to find a farrier. Do you know of anyone around here who might be able to help?"

Mr Jackson's attention shifted to a blue van which had turned into the drive and was heading towards the stables. "What a piece of luck!" he remarked.

The van stopped and a short, wiry man got out. "Morning, Mr Jackson, sir."

"Good morning, Peter. This young lady was wondering if I knew of a farrier who could fix her pony's loose shoe. Can you think of anyone?"

"That's a tough one, sir. The man I have in mind will do anything for a nice cup of coffee."

"I'd better put the kettle on, then," Mr Jackson replied. He turned to the riders and smiled. "Bring your horses in and tie them up over there. Peter has come to shoe Moon. He'll tap the pony's shoe on for you, no problem."

"Oh, thank you, Mr Jackson! You've saved our holiday!" Katy exclaimed.

"Don't thank me, thank Peter," Mr Jackson replied. "Now then, young lady, come and see Moon."

Moon looked fantastic. He was fat with summer grass and obviously very happy. Melanie took several photos with her mobile phone so Katy would be able to email them to Rachel.

"I keep Pixie, the pony, for the grandchildren, you know. She and Moon are great friends, aren't you, eh?" He stroked Moon's neck gently and then gave him a couple of light pats. "Right then, refreshments are called for. Follow me, girls. One coffee coming up, Peter!"

Mrs Jackson was a smart, plump, motherly lady. She

insisted they should have sandwiches with their hot drinks, as it was nearly lunchtime. It was so homely in the kitchen and the Jacksons seemed like old friends, even though they'd only just met.

The farrier knocked on the kitchen door and poked his head round. "All done and ready to go," he said cheerfully.

They thanked Mrs Jackson and went outside again.

"Thank you so much. How much do I owe you?" Melanie asked Mr Jackson.

"Nothing. Put it on my bill, Peter, there's a good chap." He said firmly.

"Oh, it's much too kind of you."

"Not another word! It's my pleasure!" said Mr Jackson, holding Melanie's horse for her as she mounted. "So nice to see the young enjoying themselves properly. None of this addiction to the telly which seems to plague so many children these days."

Katy and Alice smiled knowingly at each other, thinking of their late night TV session in the hotel.

"Remember, past the pub, up the lane and you'll get to Winsford Hill," Mr Jackson called as the riders clattered out of his yard. "Good luck!"

"Thank you!" they shouted back.

"Now, that's what I call a real gentleman," Melanie declared.

Katy rode up alongside. "Yes, I can't wait to tell

Rachel," she said. "Can you send me the photos you took of Moon when we get home, so I can email them to her?"

"Yes, of course," said Melanie, smiling down at her. "I've been taking plenty of pictures, so I'll send you a whole heap of them. Then Rachel will be able to see what you've been up to."

"I'll show them to Trifle as well, so she can see what fun we'll have when I'm riding her," Katy said.

"Don't be daft!" Alice chipped in from behind. "Ponies don't understand photographs."

Katy swivelled round in her saddle. "How d'you know? I think Trifle understands lots of things she's not supposed to." Then, remembering something Rachel had said, she added triumphantly, "Never underestimate an Exmoor pony."

Melanie laughed. "Quite right! Everyone okay for a trot up the hill?"

"Yes!" the girls replied, glad to end the conversation.

Max, Melanie's chestnut hunter, was seventeen hands high. He powered up the hill, covering the ground in long, easy strides while the girls' ponies did their best to keep up. Their metal shoes played a tune on the tarmac, the steady thud of Max's hooves interspersed with the hasty clatter of Shannon and Jacko's.

*

B y the time the riders reached the open moorland of Winsford Hill, the sun had broken through the mist. The penalty for this was that insects buzzed around. The horses shook their heads, swished their tails and stamped their feet with irritation.

The views from the top of the hill were spectacular, with the sun shining through the remaining wisps of mist. Several Exmoor pony mares and foals were grazing nearby, making the most of a slight breeze which gave them some relief from the flies. Melanie took a few photos.

"If I were a painter I'd paint landscapes like this," Katy said.

"Don't be so modest," said Alice. "You're a brilliant painter. Your pictures are always being put up on the classroom wall." She hesitated, realising she was straying dangerously close to the forbidden subject of school, and then went on, "You'll send Katy those photos you've just taken, won't you, Mum? Then she can paint them."

"Certainly, but I'm afraid they won't do justice to this scenery," Melanie said. "You'd better try to remember it as well, Katy."

They rode on, passing near the mares and foals but not close enough to disturb them. Katy couldn't help remembering Trifle as a foal on the moorland above Barton Farm, wandering as she pleased without a care in the world. I'm sure, if she could choose, she'd want to be wild and free on the moor, Katy thought with a twinge of guilt. There and then, she made a promise to Trifle that one day she'd set her free again. Then she could be with her family, roaming the open moor and having babies of her own.

"I know all Exmoor ponies look pretty much the same," Alice said, "but these ones look different from yours at Barton, somehow. I can't really put my finger on it. They're smaller and narrower, aren't they? With prettier heads."

Katy couldn't think what to say to that, so she said nothing. Alice Gardner, you really can be unbelievably rude sometimes, she thought. Fancy saying these ponies are prettier than Trifle!

Alice looked uncomfortable. "I mean, everything looks a bit different on this part of Exmoor, doesn't it? Take the moorland, for example. Our common has much shorter heather and more grass. This is more scrubby, and the heather's all twiggy. It'd be difficult to gallop flat-out here like we do at home, wouldn't it?"

"Suppose so," said Katy, and they fell into an awkward silence.

They rode off the hill and into a wood, where the flies were so bad that Melanie dismounted, unpacked her rucksack, found the repellent and sprayed the horses with it. Most of the flies kept their distance after that.

The bridle path along the river valley to Withypool was beautiful. Sunlight danced in dapples through the trees and glistened on the water as it flowed past. They rode along the narrow path in single file, drinking in the peaceful sights and sounds of the riverbank.

Despite the tranquil setting, Katy couldn't help mulling over how annoying Alice had become. Deep down, she realised that the more she convinced herself she didn't like Alice the less she liked herself and the more miserable she became. It was what Granfer would have called a vicious circle. She didn't know what to do. The sun shone, the birds sang and Katy found herself counting the hours until she'd be home.

Near the village, they crossed the river and went up a track onto open moorland. From there it was a short distance to the farm where they were staying that night. It belonged to a lady called Mrs Soames.

It turned out that Mrs Soames was a good friend of Granfer's. She bred Exmoor ponies as well, and in what she called "the glory days" she and Granfer had been amicable rivals in the show ring. Katy took to her immediately. She was a bird-like little lady, with deeply tanned skin and wispy grey hair partially captured by several grips. Her grey-blue eyes were wise, kind and perceptive, and they regarded Katy with an intensity she found rather unnerving.

Mrs Soames lived in a sort of controlled, comfortable chaos. There was not a lot of difference between the house and the farmyard – many of the animals seemed to have free range in both – but everything was surprisingly clean despite being cluttered.

They cooked sausages and beef burgers on a barbecue for supper. Then Melanie went inside to have a bath and Mrs Soames drove the girls in an old pick-up truck to see her ponies on Withypool Common. They found the herd, and got out of the vehicle to take a closer look.

"These ponies are different again," said Alice.

Mrs Soames looked interested. "How do you mean, Alice?"

Alice glanced at Katy. "Well, I mean different herds seem to look different somehow," she said uncertainly.

Katy sighed. Here we go again, she thought.

"You're very observant, Alice," Mrs Soames said. "Over the years, moorland breeders have encouraged certain characteristics which they admire, so now each herd has a distinctive look. I've always favoured the larger, broader, lighter-coloured ponies myself. And, Katy, your grandfather seems to like a similar type, but darker. We're both very keen to breed the traditional type of Exmoor with a good strong jaw and a deep body. It makes them rather less attractive than the pretty little show-pony types which are preferred by some of the judges nowadays, but it helps them survive a moorland winter. I think Exmoors need large jaws to chew up the huge amount of rough vegetation they need to eat, and large stomachs to digest it all. Some of the Exmoors you see at shows are lovely riding ponies but look as if they wouldn't last five minutes on open moorland."

"You see, Katy? That's what I meant when I said…" Alice began.

Katy felt a massive wave of emotion welling up inside her. She burst into tears, and ran back to the pick-up truck.

B it by bit, the full story of the girl's troubled friendship came out as they sat side-by-side in the cab of the truck with Mrs Soames. She listened a lot and talked a little. Gradually the ponies came closer. They stood in a circle around the vehicle, nodding their heads and swishing their tails. Behind them, the sun sank to the horizon and slowly disappeared, leaving an orange glow in the darkening sky. Stars began to appear, the windscreen steamed up and it became chilly, but still Katy and Alice kept talking, as if a dam had broken and words were flooding out. They probably would have stayed until midnight if Mrs Soames hadn't suggested hot chocolate.

Later, as the girls climbed into their beds, Alice said, "I'm really sorry, Katy."

"What for?" Katy asked. "I'm the one who should be sorry. The more we talked with Mrs Soames, the more I realised how unfair I've been. Perhaps I'd decided not to like you so I wouldn't miss you or something, so a part of me was *trying* to get annoyed with you the whole time, if you see what I mean. Oh, I don't know. I'm sorry if I've ruined the holiday. I feel like an ungrateful pig."

Alice grinned. "Now you're being unfair to pigs!"

Katy threw her pillow at Alice.

"Ow!" she said, and threw it back. She turned off the bedside light. "Friends for ever?"

"Friends for ever."

"Night, Katy."

"Night, Alice."

There was a pause, then they both started giggling and talking. They eventually fell asleep just before dawn.

Katy felt happier than she'd been for ages as they set off on the final day of their ride. Soon the early morning mist gave way to blue sky, clouds like cotton wool and just enough breeze to keep the insects away. The air was so clear that distant hills seemed close enough to touch. The atmosphere between Katy and Alice had cleared too. The resentment which had clouded their friendship for many months had evaporated.

Melanie didn't say anything about it, but Katy could see she knew what had happened and was glad. Perhaps she'd secretly hoped that the ride would help the girls sort out their differences. If so, Katy had yet another reason to be grateful to her.

They skirted around the top of some moorland, dropped down to cross a stream and joined a road leading to an ancient bridge called Landacre. It was only eleven-thirty when they got there, but it was so beautiful and the pools beside the bridge looked so cool and inviting that they stopped for a paddle. Soon day trippers in their cars started to arrive, so they rode on towards Simonsbath where they paused for sandwiches and ice creams.

They were almost on home ground again, with just one range of hills to cross. The hilltops formed a broad, flat, boggy expanse covered with rushes, bog plants and rough grasses.

Katy gazed at the sepia-coloured landscape spread out before her. "All the colours up here are the colours of Exmoor ponies: dark browns, light browns, golds and blond bits all mixed together. If I brought Trifle up here, she'd become invisible!"

"You're quite right, Katy. Exmoor ponies are incredibly well-camouflaged, aren't they? Just as nature intended," agreed Melanie.

The ground oozed water with every step they took, like a sponge being squeezed.

"Boggy ground gives me the creeps," Alice remarked.

"It's always good to be wary of it," Melanie said. "A pretty good rule of thumb is to avoid tall reeds and cotton grass, like that stuff over there, and also anything that's bright green and mossy. If we stick to these tracks we'll be okay, I hope."

The girls followed Melanie and Max along the soft, peaty path which ran like a dark ribbon through the tall grasses, occasionally meandering round a boggy area or widening out into soggy hollows which had to be skirted around.

After a while the ground started to dip away and became firmer. The view in front of them was amazing, like a living map. A patchwork of moorland and farms stretched to the coast, with the sea shimmering beyond. Further still, the blue-grey hills of South Wales merged with a distant skyline.

The riders stopped for a while to get their bearings, picking out the distant clusters of buildings and familiar field patterns that were Barton Farm and Stonyford, separated by the purple and brown moorland of the Common.

"Aren't we lucky to live here?" Melanie said.

Katy and Alice grinned at each other.

At that moment, Katy felt like the luckiest person in the world.

5

Show Shine

Exford Show took place a few days after Katy came back from her riding holiday. In a rash moment several months earlier, Katy had entered Trifle for two in-hand Exmoor pony classes. She still wanted to go, even though she knew she'd be competing against the best and she hadn't had nearly enough time to prepare. Exford was the main show for Exmoor ponies, and people travelled from far and wide to take part.

As Melanie would be taking Trifle to the show with Promise, Max, and Alice's show pony, Bella, she suggested that Jacko and Trifle should both stay at

Stonyford, which suited Katy fine. It was much more fun getting everything ready with Alice and Melanie to help her.

B y the night before, Katy was feeling quite hopeful. Trifle had done a pretty good mock show in front of Melanie, Penny and Alice that afternoon, and it was now time for the beauty parlour.

"I wonder why they don't call in-hand classes leading rein classes. In-hand sounds as if you're carrying the pony, not leading it," Katy said.

Alice rubbed frothy shampoo into Bella's coat. "I suppose it's because leading rein classes are for children who are being led, so they have to call classes with no riders something else."

"Trifle's already growing her winter coat, you know. Look how long it is!" Katy said, ruffling the dense mat on her pony's back. As she did so, lots of dusty flecks appeared. "Oh no! Look at all this dandruff coming out! What on earth am I going to do?"

"Here, use some of this," Alice replied, handing her the bottle of shampoo.

"I don't know. Granfer always says you shouldn't shampoo an Exmoor pony because it destroys the waterproofing in their coat. He says shampooing is the lazy man's way out and he always marks down washed ponies if he's judging. To make a pony really shine you have to brush it regularly, according to him."

"He's probably right, but you've left it a bit late for regular brushing now, haven't you? That shampoo doesn't smell of anything much, so I bet the judge won't be able to tell. Look at it this way: it's that or a scruffy, scurfy pony," Alice said.

Trifle didn't like being washed much. She clamped her tail against her body and looked grumpy. Rain was forecast overnight, so they kept the ponies stabled.

Katy stayed in Alice's room. Needless to say, neither of them got much sleep. Katy must have drifted off sometime, because she woke with dreams of rosettes and shiny cups in her head.

Perhaps it's a sign, and my dreams will come true today, she thought. There was a spring in her step as she went to give Trifle some breakfast. She opened the stable door. "Oh, no! Trifle's gone all fluffy! I *knew* I shouldn't have shampooed her!"

Alice appeared in the doorway, and started giggling. "Talk about a bad hair day!"

"It isn't funny, Alice! What am I going to *do*?" Katy wailed.

Alice went into the tack room and came out clutching a spray can. "A potion for every problem!" she said grandly.

Katy groaned.

"Trust me! This works like magic! Look, it says *Magic Show Shine*. Does just what it says on the tin. I use it all the time on Bella and Shannon. It makes their coats really smooth."

Trifle wasn't at all impressed by the noise of the spray can, so Katy resorted to spaying lots of it onto a sponge and then wiping her with it. The result was rather streaky, and she used up the whole tin, but it seemed to have the desired effect of laying Trifle's hair down smoothly against her body.

A final brush and tidy up, a check through everything in the lorry and they were ready to go! Katy felt jittery with excitement.

Her high hopes vanished as soon as they drove into the showground. Everywhere she looked there were well-behaved, immaculately turned out Exmoor ponies.

"I thought they were supposed to be a rare breed!" Alice joked.

"So did I. Perhaps they're all here," Katy replied, trying to smile. She didn't feel very jokey, though. If anything, she felt a bit sick. Her nerves were made worse by the sight of Granfer and Mrs Soames chatting outside the Exmoor Pony Society tent. Granfer caught sight of the Stonyford lorry, and waved.

By the time Melanie had parked the lorry, Granfer and Mrs Soames were by the ramp, waiting expectantly.

After they'd all greeted each other, Mrs Soames said, "I can't wait to see the famous Trifle!"

"Well, I'm afraid you'll have to wait a little while, because she'll be the last out. We loaded her first to give Promise a lead," Melanie said.

Max, then Bella, then Promise emerged one by one down the ramp of the lorry like models walking down a catwalk. They were stylish and confident, with travel rugs, plaited manes, tail protectors and leg boots.

Finally, it was Trifle's turn. Katy hurried into the lorry, released the catch of the partition and gasped, "Oh, no!"

If it hadn't been so awful, it would have been funny. Trifle's coat must have been rubbing against the partitions, and the large quantities of *Magic Show Shine* which Katy had sponged into it earlier appeared to have set hard in lots of little spikes. Trifle looked like a hedgehog!

Alice, Melanie and Mrs Soames all saw the funny side, and busied themselves trying to brush the show shine out of Trifle's hair. Granfer, however, didn't look at all amused. He walked away, saying he'd fetch Katy's showing number for her.

All the activity on the showground – unfamiliar horses and ponies everywhere, the crackly loudspeaker, lots of people, flags flapping in the breeze and children running around with metallic balloons on sticks – made Trifle unusually excitable. She became even worse when Katy tried to lead her away from the Stonyford lorry to the show ring.

There were fifteen ponies in the class, and Trifle was the worst behaved by far. She was permanently bent towards Katy as she jogged and side-stepped around the ring, tossing her head and anxiously whinnying for her travelling companions. Her coat became sweaty and stuck up in untidy spikes again.

When they lined up for their individual shows, Trifle fidgeted and barged into her neighbours, upsetting the whole line like a row of dominoes. Eventually the moment Katy had been dreading arrived: it was their turn. Her hands and arms ached, but she doggedly stuck to the routine they'd practised at Stonyford, including trotting past the judge. It was then that disaster struck. Worn out with the effort of controlling Trifle for so long, Katy missed her footing and fell over, letting go of the lead rope as she did so.

Trifle took fright and bolted out of the ring, scattering spectators as she fled. Her urgent whinnies were answered by Promise, whose in-hand hunter class had just lined up in the main ring. Overjoyed to hear her friend, Trifle galloped towards her, avoiding several people who tried to stop her, and found the entrance to the collecting ring. Dodging past the stewards, she charged into the large arena, amidst gasps from the spectators. The orderly line-up of show hunters disintegrated into chaos until one of the stewards eventually managed to catch her.

"At least nobody was hurt," Alice said, putting a comforting arm round Katy's shoulders as they sat on the lorry ramp.

Trifle, now tied up securely behind a partition, had settled down in the familiar surroundings of the lorry and was munching away at her haynet.

Katy blew her nose and rubbed her hot, tear-swollen eyes. "I suppose," she said. "Oh, I feel such an *idiot!*"

"Perhaps you do now, but I bet you'll be joking about it soon. I mean, embarrassing things happen to everyone, especially with horses."

Katy sniffed as she watched some perfectly behaved Exmoor ponies trotting by on their way to a class. "I bet nothing this awful has ever happened to you."

"Okay, how about this, then. When I was about five Mum dressed me up as Humpty Dumpty for a fancy dress competition on Misty. He wore an old sheet painted like a wall, and I was perched on top. Mum had made my costume out of a hardened beach ball, so I was completely round and I could hardly move.

Anyway, a gust of wind made the sheet flap like crazy, and poor old Misty was terrified. He pulled away from Mum and fled out of the ring, with me clinging on for dear life. There were lots of smart horses waiting in the collecting ring for some sort of parade, and they all bolted in different directions when a flapping four-legged wall with a screaming round thing on top hurtled towards them."

Katy couldn't help smiling.

"So at least you weren't dressed as Humpty Dumpty," Alice added.

The two friends looked at each other, and burst out laughing.

6

Testing Times

The rest of the summer holidays raced by. Katy spent as much time as possible at Stonyford, helping out in return for lessons and lifts to Pony Club events, but she also worked at home whenever she could, making beds and cleaning the house for her mum's bed and breakfast business in return for pocket money. By the end of the holidays she had enough to buy what she'd been saving up for since May. Tom took her into town and helped her choose from the many different deals on offer.

All too soon, it was nearly the autumn term, and the day Alice was leaving to stay with her dad before going to boarding school. Katy helped to load the lorry with Alice's possessions and, last but not least, Shannon. "It looks as if you're going on a world trek!" she said.

"Feels like it too," Alice replied, smiling bravely. It was a shock to see her eyes brimming with tears. She hardly ever cried.

"Hey, you're always the cheerful one! Please don't cry, or you'll start me off." Katy pulled her brand new phone out of her pocket, still revelling in the feel of it. "Look what I've bought, so we can keep in touch easily. See? Your mobile number's the first on my list."

"That's great! But I thought there wasn't any signal at Barton." Alice quickly brushed away a tear which had escaped and was trickling down her cheek.

"Not at the farm, no. But Tom's shown me the best places to get a signal. Up by the Common gate's good, so I'll go there every evening to phone you.

Alice couldn't hold back her tears any longer. "It'll be odd knowing you're there while I'm miles away. Oh, I'm going to miss you *so* much!"

The two girls hugged each other.

"I'll miss you as well, but it'll soon be half term," Katy replied, trying to sound upbeat. She was counting the days already, and not just because she'd see Alice again. Melanie had promised that at half term she'd help her to ride Trifle for the first time. "It's only six weeks and two days away," she added.

"That sounds like ages to me. A lot can happen in six weeks," Alice said.

Unfortunately, she was right.

The first thing which happened to Katy was her new school. It was a dreary maze of rain-stained concrete, grubby glass and peeling light-green paintwork, and it was miles away from Barton Farm. Her old primary school seemed cosy and quaint. It had been so easy there; she'd been one of the oldest and Alice had been her best friend. Now she was one of the youngest and smallest, and there was no Alice.

Katy spent her first week in a daze, swimming through a sea of unrecognisable names and anonymous faces, too stressed to take it all in. She seemed to be permanently confused about where she should be and what she should be doing. Another hassle was the endless tests all the new students had to take. She did so badly in those that she was streamed into the lowest class for most subjects. Claire and most of the other girls she knew from her old school were in the higher classes, so Katy often found herself alone with nobody to latch onto. Gradually she got to know people, but she had a feeling none of them would become really close – not like Alice, anyway. As far as Katy was concerned, Alice was still her best friend, although it didn't help to hear that her new school was "magic" and she'd made "loads of friends". When she spoke to Alice on the telephone, there were usually girls giggling in the background. She couldn't help feeling jealous.

After a while Katy's school life settled into a relentless, tiring rhythm. There were a few things she looked forward to though, and the highlight of every week was a double art lesson. Their first task was to paint a picture titled "summer holidays". Katy painted a picture of the view she'd seen from Winsford Hill on her riding holiday, with ponies grazing in the foreground and mist rising from the valleys. The art teacher thought it was so good that he helped her make a frame for it. Katy decided she'd give it to her dad for his birthday.

Unexpectedly, Katy's other favourite lesson was a regular session with the learning support teacher, Mr Bayliss. He gave Katy even more tests and told her she was dyslexic. "It's complicated," he said. "Basically it means you find it difficult to read and write but you're much better than most people at practical things."

"I could have told you that without any tests at all!" Katy said.

Mr Bayliss laughed. "You must be very bright to have got this far through the education system without anyone discovering your dyslexia," he said. "But the good news is we know about it now, and there's plenty I can do to help."

"Does that mean if I work hard I'll be able to get into higher classes for things like biology and geography?" Katy asked.

He leaned back in his chair, took his glasses off and beamed at her. "Highly likely. Shall we make that our goal?"

"Yes please!" said Katy. She'd really enjoyed those subjects at her old school, and her ride across Exmoor in the summer had made her even more interested in the countryside around her. She had a secret dream of one day becoming a National Park warden.

"Excellent!" said Mr Bayliss, "I can see we're going to get along famously."

Despite her resolution, Katy found it hard to set aside enough time for homework in the evenings, what with looking after Trifle and Jacko plus keeping in touch with Alice at her boarding school and Rachel in Australia. There was one computer at Barton Farm, on a desk in the corner of the kitchen. Katy's mum often found her chatting to Alice or Rachel on Facebook rather than getting on with her homework.

Like Alice, Rachel seemed to be having a good time. The photos she posted on her page were of deep blue skies, sun-bleached gum trees and vast, arid landscapes. It looked like a different planet. In return,

Katy sent photos from her mobile of the house, the family and, of course, the ponies.

Then one day, out of the blue, Rachel sent some terrible news:

> *Dear Katy, I don't know how to tell you this, but the most awful thing has happened – Moon's dead. Mr Jackson lent him to someone (actually, the lady who took that photo you've got of me on Moon) because he had to go into hospital for a hip operation. She contacted him a couple of days ago to say Moon had died in some sort of accident. Desperately sad. Wish I'd never left. Miss you all v badly. Lots of love, Rachel X*

Katy hardly slept at all that night. She kept thinking about Moon, and Rachel grieving on the other side of the world, and how she'd feel if she lost Jacko or Trifle. The possibility had never occurred to her before. One thing was for certain: she'd never sell them. Never in a million years.

With its warm Aga and large table, the kitchen was the room where everyone gathered to talk or work. Mum did the farm accounts and records on the kitchen table or at the computer, and Dad often did his painting there in the evening. Art had always been Dad's hobby, but since they'd been doing bed and breakfast in the farmhouse it had become a good way of getting some extra cash as well. Dad hung his pictures on the walls, with a discreet price tag in the corner, and it was surprising how many guests bought one to remind them of their holiday.

"Thank goodness for your paintings," Katy overheard Mum saying to Dad one day when she was doing the accounts. "They've helped to make ends meet all summer, but unfortunately there won't be many visitors over the winter. If those cattle don't sell well in the autumn we'll be up the creek without a paddle." Katy didn't really know what she meant by that, but she knew it didn't sound good.

On her dad's birthday, Katy gave him the painting she'd done at school. He said it was brilliant, and he hung it in the kitchen for everyone to see. Katy decided that giving a special present to someone was one of the best feelings in the world.

Dad had never been particularly fond of sheep, but his cattle were different. They were a registered herd of Red Ruby Devons, with gentle natures and deep reddish-brown coats, and over the years they'd become his pride and joy. He knew them all by name and, like Granfer with his Exmoor ponies, he could remember the pedigree of each animal for generations. Barton

65

Devons had a good reputation, and the main income of the farm came from the sale of pedigree in-calf cows and heifers at the breed society sale every autumn.

Before they went to market, all the cattle had to be tested by the vet to make sure none of them had bovine tuberculosis, or TB as everyone called it. To control the spread of TB, there were strict laws about the movement of cattle from herds which failed the test. The Barton herd had never had the disease, but it could be spread from farm to farm by wildlife as well as farm stock. Katy could tell her dad was worried, especially as several farms in the area had come down with TB for the first time that year. She also knew that if the herd failed its test, none of the cows and heifers which Dad had booked into the big pedigree sale would be able to go, as cattle from infected herds weren't allowed.

In the week just before half term, the Barton herd had its annual TB test. One cow called Peppermint failed. For the first time ever, the Barton Herd was placed under TB restrictions, which meant all sorts of rules and regulations came into force and Dad's options for selling his cattle were severely limited. Overnight, their value had plummeted.

Katy guessed they were now up the creek without a paddle, and from the mood of her family she now had a pretty good idea of what that meant.

7

Riding Trifle

Ten days without the daily grind of school was enough of a reason to be excited about half term, but for Katy there was the added thrill of seeing Alice again and – hopefully, if all went well – riding Trifle for the first time. Katy felt fizzy with excitement whenever she thought about it.

Trifle was three-and-a-half years old. According to Melanie, that was a perfect age for a pony to be "backed", or trained to carry a rider.

"All horses and ponies are different," she'd said, "but if you back them too young, before they've finished growing, you can damage them for life. Leave it too long, though, and it can be more difficult to get them to accept the idea. Besides, if we do it in the autumn half term I'll have the time to help you. Bring both the ponies over and stay for a few days, if you want to."

Of course, Katy wanted to very much, and so it was all arranged. What she should pack and what they'd do during her stay were the subjects of many emails, text messages and phone calls between Katy and Alice for weeks beforehand.

"You're only going a couple of miles away!" Mum commented as Katy dithered about whether she should take her treasured silver photo frame.

Katy packed the frame between some clothes and zipped up her bulging rucksack. "Oh, I almost forgot! Toothbrush and toothpaste!"

Mum laughed and rolled her eyes heavenwards.

On the Monday of half term, Katy led Trifle into the outdoor school at Stonyford. Trifle was wearing the saddle and bridle which Rachel had bought for her. Katy had been tacking her up for several weeks to get her used to them, and Granfer had helped to "mouth" Trifle, or get her used to a bit in her mouth.

A casual observer seeing the pony would have thought that Trifle was a reliable riding school pony.

All the surroundings were familiar to her, so she was happy and relaxed, even though Katy's heart was pounding like a sledgehammer.

Melanie was in a dilemma. Putting a rider on a horse's back for the first time was always unpredictable and risky. Sometimes horses would explode and run away, buck or rear. More often, they planted their feet on the ground and were afraid to move. An Exmoor pony, with its primitive instincts for survival, would be more likely than most to go for the bucking option. The sensible thing to do would be to get Penny to ride Trifle to begin with. However, Melanie knew how much it would mean to Katy if she were the first person to sit on her pony. It was always an extraordinary moment, so for Katy – who'd seen Trifle as a newborn foal and had risked so much to own her – it would be the experience of a lifetime. Seeing how happy and relaxed Trifle was, Melanie made her decision. She'd let Katy choose.

"Would you like to do this, or shall I ask Penny?"

Katy wanted desperately to be the first person on Trifle's back, but the voice of reason in her head told her she might get it wrong. "I don't know. What do you think, Melanie?"

"It's entirely up to you," Melanie said, smiling uncertainly.

"I'll do it!" said Katy, before the voice of reason could shut her up.

"Okay, then. You need to be very tranquil, like a still sea on a summer's day. Can you do that for me? And remember to keep breathing, slowly and evenly. She'll get anxious if you hold your breath, because that'll show you're nervous. Ponies are very sensitive to breathing, you see. Now, when you're ready, I want you to stand by her saddle so I can give you a leg-up." Melanie's voice was clear and composed.

Katy thought about the sea, and was surprised how much it helped. Her thumping heart slowed down and she felt much more relaxed as she stood looking at the saddle, trying her best to breathe steadily.

"Now, the same rules apply here as for handling her on the ground. Sure, positive movements, okay? I'm going to give you a leg-up and I want you to gently lie across the saddle. Don't put your foot in the stirrup and don't try to swing your leg over. Just lie there for a little while and then slide off again. Bear in mind that Trifle may get worried when she sees you above her, especially when you appear over on the other side. If she starts getting really agitated, slip off quickly – feet first rather than head first, of course!" Melanie said, taking hold of Katy's left leg. "Right. On the count of three, then: one, two, three."

As slowly and carefully as she could, Katy held onto the saddle and lifted herself up and over, so she was lying across Trifle's back. It was horribly uncomfortable, and she found it difficult not to hold her breath with the top of the saddle pressing into her rib cage, but luckily Melanie didn't ask her to stay like that for long.

"Excellent. You see, all that hard work you put into getting Trifle to stand is paying off, isn't it? Now, we'll do that a few more times, and I want you to stroke her on the other flank, to get her used to having you on both sides."

Katy did that, and Melanie was so pleased with Trifle that she suggested Katy should sit astride next time, keeping her head low while swinging her right leg over the back of the saddle. "Keep your head down so it's out of her field of vision to begin with, and don't put your feet in the stirrups so you can get off quickly if you have to. Very carefully, now," Melanie said as she grasped Katy's leg yet again and lifted her up.

Katy became so absorbed in what she was doing that she forgot about everything else. It was as if the rest of the world had melted away and there was just her and Trifle.

Melanie sensed the change, and stopped giving her instructions. She just held Trifle's lead rope and watched as Katy talked to her pony in a low, soothing voice and stroked both sides of her neck while gradually sitting up in the saddle.

Trifle's ears flicked back and forth, taking it all in. She seemed slightly puzzled by the new game Katy wanted to play with her, but not at all frightened.

Eventually, Katy sat tall in the saddle and carefully put her feet in the stirrups. She'd done it!

Melanie stood by Trifle's head, beaming up at her. "Well done!" she said. Then she nodded towards the house. "You've drawn quite a crowd, look."

Katy looked. There, leaning on the gate and giving her a big thumbs up, were Alice, Penny, Josh, Rupert and ... Granfer!

"Oh, Granfer's there!" Katy said in an excited whisper. He had seen it all, and his smile was nearly as broad as his face!

"Shall we try walking over to them?" Melanie asked.

"D'you think she'll be okay?"

"She's been fine so far, and she seems quite happy. Some horses suddenly get worried when they try to move with such an unfamiliar weight on their back though, so try to stay relaxed but be prepared for anything, if that makes sense," said Melanie.

Trifle felt very wobbly and unsure of herself, but she didn't put a foot wrong as she walked with short, cautious steps towards the gate. Katy took in every detail: the pony's compact body, her chunky neck with a bushy mane cascading down both sides and her fluffy rounded ears with black tips. It's just like I'd dreamed it would be, only better, thought Katy. It's really happening! After over three years of waiting, I'm riding Trifle!

8

Life is Full of Surprises

On the last Saturday of half term, Katy, Alice, Melanie and Penny were sitting in the kitchen at Stonyford, eating a well-earned lunch. There were always lots of people booked in for rides at the weekend, so they'd had a busy morning.

"Oh, brill!" Alice said, picking up the newspaper. "Let's see what horses are for sale this week!"

It had become a Stonyford tradition to look in the *Western Morning News* each Saturday because that was the big day for horse and pony advertisements. When Melanie had been looking for horses for the riding school, they'd studied the pages in earnest. Nowadays, it was the girls' equivalent of window-shopping.

"Here's one for you, Katy! Pretty coloured mare. Unspoilt but green…"

"Yuck! I'd rather not have a green-coloured pony, thanks!" Katy joked.

"Okay, then. How about this one? Hmm, it sounds rather nice actually. 'Stunning bay seven-year-old gelding. Sixteen-three hands. Experienced hunter, dressage, cross country, show jumping. Scope to go to the top. Genuine reason for sale. Five thousand pounds or near offer.' Sounds gorgeous. Looks gorgeous too."

Katy took the paper from Alice. She couldn't believe what she was seeing. There was a small, slightly blurred photo of a horse jumping a fence. The horse was Moon, and the rider was Rachel! Katy knew because she had the same photo in her silver photo frame.

Melanie rang Mr Jackson right away to tell him that Moon was advertised in the newspaper. He was sure the lady who'd borrowed Moon couldn't possibly have been devious enough to fake his death and then sell him. However, he said his wife would drive him over to Stonyford immediately so he could see for himself.

Once Mr Jackson had seen that the two photographs

were identical, his attitude changed completely. They had to act fast.

Melanie rang the mobile number given in the advertisement and pretended she was interested in buying the horse. The man on the other end told her there was somebody going to see him early on Sunday morning, so Melanie said she'd like to see him that afternoon. "Okay, let's go! No time to lose!" she said as soon as she put down the phone.

"We could have one small problem," Mr Jackson said. "If it *is* Moon, and we need to bring him home, it could be tricky. He's not a good traveller, and he sometimes refuses to load if he's by himself. What a pity his old friend, Pixie, isn't here."

"How about Trifle?" Katy said. "We could take her! She loves travelling."

So Trifle was loaded into the Stonyford lorry and they set off, with Melanie, Alice and Katy in the lorry cab and the Jacksons following in their car. Mr Jackson didn't recognise the address. It sounded as if the horse was being sold by a dealer, but the lady who'd borrowed Moon could be there, so the plan was that the Jacksons would wait out of sight until the others were sure the horse was Moon. Of course, it was always possible that there had simply been a mistake in the paper and the wrong photo had been used. Katy didn't know what to think. A part of her wanted to believe that it was a mix-up because she couldn't imagine anyone being that dishonest, but at the same time she hoped desperately that Rachel's beloved Moon was still alive.

The dealer's yard was a ramshackle mixture of old brick stables with modern low-cost stabling squeezed in-between. A gum-chewing teenage girl with bright red hair looked up from sweeping the yard as they drove in. Before they had time to say anything, she turned and walked away.

"Charming!" Melanie commented.

"Imagine what Mr Jackson would say about her!" Alice said, and Katy giggled.

A short, wiry man appeared, smiling. He didn't look like a crook. "Park your lorry over there," he said, looking pleased. Katy guessed he liked people who turned up with lorries, as it meant they intended to buy the horse straight away. "You're the lady who rang earlier? You've come to see Comet, the horse in the paper today?"

"Yes, that's right," said Melanie.

"Can't be the same horse," Katy whispered to Alice.

"Anyone can change a name, silly!" Alice whispered back.

They followed the man along a row of looseboxes.

Several of the horses put their ears back at the visitors, and a few tried to bite them.

The man stopped by a gaunt bay animal with a runny nose. "This is Comet!" he said, as if he were introducing the winner of the Grand National.

There were no markings on the horse's face. He couldn't be Moon.

"Told you!" Katy whispered to Alice, slightly pleased that she was right but also disappointed.

Melanie obviously had to pretend she was interested. The man went into the box, tied the horse up short and took off its rugs. Katy noticed that the floor of the box was bare, except for several piles of hard droppings and a foul-smelling wet area in one corner. Some musty hay lay limply in an old haynet which had been patched up with baler twine. The horse had been blanket-clipped, and there were sore patches on his back where a badly fitting saddle had been rubbing. Melanie ran her hand lightly over the sores.

"They're nothing," the man said quickly. "Just superficial wear and tear you'd expect to find in a horse which has seen some life." He slammed the saddle roughly onto the horse's back, and the poor animal jerked his head up and flattened his ears. "Don't let his attitude in the box put you off," he continued cheerfully as he yanked up the girth. "He's totally different when he's ridden."

The red-haired girl appeared again.

"Ah, Sharon," said the man. "Put Comet through his paces, will you?"

Without a word or a smile, Sharon got on the horse and rode him round the tiny, uneven schooling area. She rode in trainers, jeans and a hooded sweatshirt, and with no hard hat. Katy and Alice whispered to each other with glee at the thought of what Melanie would say if she were at Stonyford. Melanie was very strict about safety, which included wearing proper riding boots and a hard hat. Surprisingly, the girl was a very good rider, and the horse did his best to perform well in the limited confines of the school. He cleared a high, uninviting-looking jump, cleverly dodging a pile of tyres and rusty barrels on the other side.

"I'm really looking for a hack. Could I possibly take him out for a short ride?" Melanie asked.

"Sure, but don't go too far. You can turn left-handed out of the gates there, and if you go on round the corner there's a field you can use. Would you like Sharon to come with you?"

"No, that's all right. I'll manage."

It was plain the dealer wasn't worried about Melanie taking the horse, probably because he had the Stonyford lorry in his yard as security and it was worth much more. "Enjoy yourself," he said as he held Comet for Melanie to mount. "You'll be able to have a good gallop around the edge of the field. I expect the girls would like a go too. He's anyone's ride."

"What on earth's she playing at?" Alice said to Katy as they obediently followed Melanie out of the yard.

"I don't know, but I'm a bit worried about leaving Trifle alone in the lorry," Katy replied. "She might get stolen instead!"

"Don't worry. I saw Mum locking it, and I'm sure we won't be long."

As soon as they were out of sight of the yard, Melanie jumped off the horse. "It's Moon! I knew as soon as I saw him!"

"But he's totally different! And where's his new moon?" Katy said in disbelief.

"The oldest trick in the book," Melanie said. "Hair dye seems to be in fashion round here. Come and look closely."

Katy studied the horse's face. There was a large whorl of hair between his eyes, and his forehead was a slightly darker brown than the rest of his face. The shape of a new moon was just visible.

"You girls run and get Mr Jackson for me," Melanie said.

Mr Jackson was there in no time. He looked at the horse and knew it was Moon. "Poor old chap! What have they done to you?" he murmured, running his hands over the horse's sore back and scars. He made a couple of calls on his mobile. The first was to his son, a solicitor, and the second was to the police. Then Katy and Alice were told to go and wait in the lorry cab while Mr Jackson and Melanie sorted a few things out.

The girls watched from the safety of the cab, trying to work out what was going on. The dealer was all smiles to begin with, but soon it looked as if he was arguing with Mr Jackson. Then they went into the house while Melanie stood holding Moon. Sharon, the girl with red hair, went up to Melanie. It looked as if she was offering to take Moon back to his box but Melanie refused. Sharon walked off and disappeared into one of the other stables. Then things got really exciting. Two police cars sped into the yard. Mr Jackson and the dealer came out of the house and, on seeing the police, the dealer tried to run away with a couple of policeman in hot pursuit. They soon caught him, and he was bundled into the back of a police car. It became rather boring after that, with lots of talking and paperwork.

At long last, Melanie led Moon over to the lorry. "It's all right, we can take him home now. How's Trifle?" she said.

Her words jolted Katy. "Oh no! I was so interested in what was going on, I haven't checked on her! We haven't heard her moving around at all, have we? I do hope she's still there!" With her heart thumping, she jumped out of the lorry cab and rushed round to the groom's door at the side. Please let her be there! Katy thought desperately. Please don't let her be stolen!

She needn't have worried. Trifle jumped slightly as Katy opened the door, and looked at her with dreamy eyes.

"I can't believe it! You've slept through all the fuss outside, haven't you?" Katy said, hugging her. "She's okay!" she shouted to Alice and Melanie.

"Thank goodness for that," said Melanie. "Now then, I'm going to let down the ramp. Let's see if Moon will go in. If he doesn't we'll have to think again.

Moon refused to set foot on the lorry ramp.

"Can you bring Trifle out here, so Moon can see her? Then she can give him a lead. I hope it works, because it'll soon be night time and I've left poor Penny looking after the twins yet again."

As they'd hoped, Moon and Trifle seemed to get on straight away. They led them around outside for a while, and then Trifle marched confidently up the ramp, closely followed by Moon. He whinnied anxiously when the partition was closed between them, but calmed down when he found he could still see her over the top of it.

"Good old Trifle. She's worth her weight in gold," Melanie said, closing the lorry ramp firmly.

As they drove out of the yard, Sharon came running up waving something. Melanie stopped and wound down the window.

"Here, I found Comet's, I mean New Moon's, proper passport in the office. The one you were given is a fake," she said. "Take care of him. He's something special."

Although it was nearly dark, Katy could see that she'd been crying because the makeup round her eyes had smudged. She felt very sorry for Sharon, left there all alone to pick up the pieces.

Mr Jackson said he'd pay Melanie full livery for Moon for a month or so, and then they'd decide what to do next.

"My specialist has told me that I can ride only if I promise not to fall off. The man obviously doesn't know the first thing about horses!" Mr Jackson said. "When Moon has been restored to his old self, we'll have to see if we can find him a really good, permanent home where he can stay for the rest of his life. I owe it to the old boy after all he's been through."

Katy decided not to tell her family about Moon until he was looking better. She didn't want Granfer to see him in such a state. In another month she would send a surprise email and photo to Rachel, and perhaps

Rachel would decide to keep Moon and transport him to Australia.

Moon was kept away from the other horses in the large foaling box behind the main stable yard because he seemed to have a cold, so the vet had advised he should be isolated for the time being.

Luckily, Trifle hadn't caught anything. She and Jacko had returned to Barton Farm the day after Moon's rescue. Katy was keen to keep riding Trifle now that she'd started, but she needed Melanie's help to get things right, so it was agreed that every Sunday she'd take Trifle over to Stonyford for a riding lesson in return for working at the stables for the rest of the day. Sunday was Penny's day off, so there was lots to do.

On the second Sunday after half term, Katy was mucking out Moon's box at Stonyford. He was tied up to a wall nearby, staring vacantly at the bricks in front of him and coughing occasionally.

Melanie walked past on her way to the house, and paused to stroke Moon's neck. "Poor thing! He's existing, not living, isn't he? If he were a human, I'd send him to a doctor to be treated for depression."

Moon's head shot up. He looked into the distance and pricked his ears.

Katy smiled. "It's the threat of a doctor. Works every time with me as well," she said.

Melanie laughed as she went to the house. Katy

83

looked at Moon and wondered why he had become so alert all of a sudden. A few minutes later, she heard a car drive into the car park. Moon whinnied and pawed the ground.

"Melanie!" Katy called, but there was no reply from the house. "Oh, bother!" she muttered. She hated dealing with visitors, and she didn't want to leave Moon because he'd become so ridiculously excited about something. Katy went round the corner to the stable yard.

A slim, sun-tanned lady got out of a red car. She looked very familiar somehow, but Katy couldn't think why.

The lady raised her hand in greeting. "Hi there, Katy!"

"Rachel!" Katy raced over to her aunt and gave her a big hug. "What *on earth* are you doing here?"

"It's a long story. Australia was great in some ways but, once the novelty had worn off, Mark and I realised how much we longed for Exmoor. I suppose we didn't realise how important our families and friends were until we didn't have them."

"The sunshine must have been amazing, though. You're as brown as an Exmoor pony!"

"I'll take that as a compliment, because it's coming from you!" Rachel said. "The funny thing is that we both missed the rain terribly."

"Oh, this is amazing! Have you and Mark come back to Exmoor for good, then?"

"Yes, we're back where we belong. I'm just so cross with myself for throwing away my dream job and my dream horse."

"Well, this is the place where dreams come true!" Katy smiled with pleasure and took Rachel by the hand. "Come and meet someone!"

"Katy, I really don't want to meet anyone at the moment. I just popped in to see you and Trifle. I'm still a bit jet-lagged and I'm in no mood for a polite conversation."

"Ah, this chap isn't very good at polite conversations either, Rachel. He's tall, dark and handsome, and I know you'll like him!"

Rachel reluctantly followed her round the corner, and stopped. "It can't be," she said huskily. "I thought he was dead."

"I know, so did we. He's alive and well, though. Well, he's sort of well, anyway. Oh, it's a long story, but it really is him, Rachel. It's Moon!"

Moon looked at Rachel, gave a low, rumbling whinny and tugged at the rope which held him, anxious to be with her.

She rushed over and hugged him, burying her face in his mane and breathing in the smell of him.

"I told you you'd like him!" Katy said.

Rachel smiled at her with trembling lips. "Thank you! I'm so happy I don't know what to do with myself!"

Moon bent round and nuzzled Rachel. At last he was happy too. Rachel was the best medicine in the world for him.

9

Trifle to the Rescue

In spite of the wonderful news about Moon, the Squires family did not have a happy Christmas. They all knew it would be their last at Barton Farm. The bank wouldn't lend Dad any more money, so the only option left was to sell the farm.

Katy hadn't dared to ask what would happen to Trifle and Jacko if her family moved to somewhere without any land. To add to her woes, Jacko lost a shoe in his muddy field and trod on the upturned nails. He was so lame he could barely walk. The vet had to come out to see him three times. It was likely that Jacko would be lame for several months and would need a great deal of care because the wounds had to be kept clean and dry. Dad was very upset when the vet's bill arrived.

It seemed to Katy that her whole world was falling apart. Barton Farm was the only home she'd ever known. Overnight, the rock on which her life had been built had turned to quicksand and the whole family was sinking.

Granfer refused to talk to Dad. Tom refused to come home. Dad and Mum were miserable. Katy was afraid to say or do anything for fear of making things worse.

Katy's goal of winning lots of rosettes and trophies at shows seemed so foolish and unimportant now. Her only wish was that somehow they would be able to keep the farm and the ponies. Without Barton her family would fall apart.

Every year, on two consecutive dawns in the winter, the Exmoor District Deer Management Society conducted a census of the red deer. A weekend was picked, and knowledgeable people were appointed to count the number of deer on their part of Exmoor.

Granfer was the person for the Barton Farm area. As he set off on a cold, misty Saturday morning, he knew that this would be his last deer count. It would also be the last calving and lambing, and the farm would probably be sold before the summer jobs came round again. If he dwelled on it too much it would break his heart.

Katy's parents had gone to see the bank manager, and she was alone in the house. She planned to watch a bit of television and then go out for a ride on Trifle. She ended up staying inside for longer than she'd meant to, as her favourite programme, *Pure Gold Pets*, was on. It was about children's pets who had done particularly heroic or funny things, and Katy had watched every single episode.

The clock in the hall struck eleven. Katy finally got dressed in jeans, short riding boots, a sweatshirt and the warm, waterproof riding coat that Rachel had given her for Christmas. As she tacked up Trifle, she realised Granfer hadn't come back from counting deer. He'd probably stopped to chat with someone. She decided to ride Trifle out towards the moor. Hopefully she'd meet him coming home.

At first Katy wasn't too concerned, but after an hour or so she began to worry. The misty weather wasn't ideal for spotting deer or people. She started calling, but her voice seemed to be soaked up by the damp air. I'll call one more time and then go home for help, she thought. Granfer may have gone home by a different route anyway.

It was Trifle who heard him. She stopped and pricked her ears.

Katy listened but couldn't hear anything. "Granfer!" she called.

"Heeeeerrrre!" came a faint reply.

Katy kept calling and following the sound. Then she stopped, horrified by what she saw. The quad bike was at the bottom of a steep valley. It was tipped on its side over a stream, and it looked as if Granfer was pinned underneath. Her knees turned to jelly, and she felt sick with fear. "Hang on, Granfer! I'm coming!" Katy shouted as she jumped off Trifle and led her, slipping and sliding, down the bank.

Granfer was conscious, but he was very cold and in a great deal of pain. "I can't feel my left leg, Katy. It's pinned under the bike. Can you get it off me?"

Katy looked around for somewhere to tie Trifle, but there was nothing. Hopefully she'll remember all those early training sessions when I taught her to stand still, Katy thought. "Stand!" she said in a stern voice.

Trifle stood.

She went over to the quad bike and heaved with all her might. It shifted slightly, then settled even more firmly in the bank.

Granfer groaned with pain.

Tears of exertion and frustration ran down Katy's cheeks. "It's no good, Granfer! It won't budge!" She stood for a second, getting her breath back, paralysed by indecision. Of course, she thought. My mobile! Thank goodness I remembered to bring it. She pulled it out of her coat pocket and switched it on. No signal. She'd have to get out of the valley. She mounted Trifle and rode her as fast as she could up the hill.

Still no signal. "Stay there, Granfer! I'll have to ride home for help!" she called.

"No! Please don't. Use Trifle." Granfer replied in a weird, far-away voice.

Katy wasn't sure what he'd said. She tried to ride Trifle back down again, but the little pony became nervous and Katy was afraid she'd fall over, so she got off and led her. "What did you say, Granfer?" she asked when she reached him.

"Can't hang on for much longer. Feel as if I'm about to pass out. Use Trifle. She'll do it," Granfer said weakly, gasping for air after each short sentence.

"How?"

"She'll pull the bike off. Make harness from that baler twine. There – on the bike. It's worth a try. Please try!"

Katy could see that Granfer was shivering violently.

She took a great handful of baler twine, which had been looped over the handlebars of the bike. She remembered from a television programme about emergency rescues that it was a good idea to talk to seriously injured people to keep them conscious. "I bet you won't tell Dad off again for leaving baler twine on the bike!" she said to Granfer, as she tried to wind and knot the orange strands into a rope. She knew that it was a particularly poor joke, because Granfer hardly said anything to Dad nowadays. Then she took the stirrup leathers off the saddle, looped one round Trifle's neck and linked the other one to it, leaving the stirrups on for a bit of extra length. Her hands were trembling so much she could hardly manage the buckles. "Good girl, Trifle. Stand still now," she said over again, trying to reassure herself as much as the pony.

Finally, Katy tied the baler twine rope to the end stirrup and led her down to the quad bike. Trifle had seen the bike many times before, but this time it looked odd and smelled strongly of the petrol which had leaked out and was floating downstream in shimmering, multi-coloured streaks. Wide-eyed, she stretched her neck out and snorted at the upturned bike.

Katy turned Trifle round so that she was facing uphill, with the bike behind her. From this position the temptation to bolt for home would be very strong.

"Stand!" Katy commanded. She passed the end of the rope across the petrol tank of the bike and tied it to the front rack on the other side. She glanced at Granfer and forced herself to smile.

He did his best to smile back. His lips had turned blue.

Now for the moment of truth. Katy went to Trifle's head and took one rein in each hand. She walked backwards slowly – trying not to fall on the slippery, uneven ground – and said, "Walk on!" in what she hoped was a firm, encouraging voice.

Trifle walked towards her and then stopped abruptly as she felt the pressure of the stirrup leather digging into her neck.

Katy took her coat off and wrapped it around the stirrup leather to act as padding. "Walk on!" she said again. Trifle walked a few paces and then stopped. Katy had an awful feeling that it wasn't going to work. "Walk on, Trifle!" She pulled hard on the reins.

Trifle plunged forwards, nearly knocking Katy off her feet. There was a crash as the quad bike turned over. The pony started to bound up the hill with alarm, but almost immediately came to a shivering halt, grounded by the dead weight of the bike.

"Good girl!" Katy said, stroking Trifle, trying to calm them both. What should she do now? She couldn't untie Trifle yet in case the bike ran back into the stream, squashing Granfer. "Stand!" she said again, remembering Rachel's words: *It's really useful if a horse stands still on command... In fact, there are situations where it could make the difference between life and death*. A year had passed since she'd said that. It felt like a lifetime.

Amazingly, Trifle stood as still as a statue while Katy hurried to the bike and wedged it with rocks from the stream. The water was icy-cold on her hands, so she definitely didn't want to get her feet wet. Why didn't I wear wellies rather than these short riding boots, she wondered. She knew the answer: Melanie always said it was dangerous to ride in wellies because they could easily get stuck in stirrups, leading to all sorts of nasty accidents.

The stream was too wide to jump over, so Katy untied the makeshift harness, put the stirrup leathers back on the saddle, mounted Trifle and rode her to Granfer on the opposite bank. Cold, wet clothes clung to his frail, gnarled body, and his skin seemed drained of life. Somehow, using all her remaining strength, she helped him to his feet, or rather to one foot. His left leg was soaking, completely numb and useless. There was no way that he'd be able to walk, and the bike was too badly damaged to be of use.

"Do you think you'd be able to ride Trifle?" Katy asked.

"Worth a try." Katy could hardly hear Granfer's thin voice through his chattering teeth.

She rode Trifle into the stream, got off on the bank and asked her to stand. The brave pony did her best to stand on the hard, slippery stones while the icy water rushed around her legs. Katy helped Granfer to lie across the saddle – using the bank as a mounting block – and then turn carefully towards Trifle's head and ease his good leg over her rump so that he was sitting astride her. It reminded Katy of how she'd sat on Trifle's back for the first time. Thank goodness Granfer's small, thought Katy. If he were tall, like Mark or Greg, Trifle wouldn't be able to carry him.

There was a ford upstream where the bank was worn down and a path crossed the stream. Katy led Trifle there, one cautious step after another, so she could get out without having to jump up the bank. Once they were all on dry ground, she tried to make Granfer as comfortable as possible. She took off her coat and put it over his shoulders in an attempt to hold in any remaining heat. As she did so, she felt cold damp air seeping through her thin sweatshirt.

She decided to follow the path leading away from home and towards Furzewater Farm, which was owned by an elderly couple called Mr and Mrs Huxtable. Furzewater was about twenty minutes away but Barton would take over an hour to reach. Katy had ridden to Furzewater several times in good weather. She hoped she'd be able to find it in the mist.

Trifle walked slowly. She seemed to know she had a very fragile passenger. As they made their way up the track, Granfer slumped forwards onto Trifle's neck.

"Granfer! Are you okay? Oh, please speak to me!" Katy cried in anguish. She was walking on Trifle's near side and holding Granfer steady with her hand on his leg, like she did when she was leading very small children at Stonyford so they wouldn't fall off.

"Warm," came a muffled response. Granfer's face was buried in Trifle's bushy mane and his arms clung to her fluffy neck. Trifle balanced her unfamiliar load carefully.

Every now and then, Katy stopped and pulled her mobile out of her jeans pocket, hoping desperately for a signal, but it was no good. She'd almost given up trying when at last she got one. It was such a shock that for a moment she couldn't decide who to ring. Then, automatically, she rang home.

The answerphone clicked on, and Katy hung up. For the first time in her life she'd have to ring the emergency services. It was scary, but the thought of what would happen if she didn't was worse.

With trembling fingers, she dialled the number. Contact with the outside world at last! An incredibly calm voice at the other end asked which service she required – police, fire or ambulance?

She felt like shouting, "Don't you know this is an

emergency?" But she said, "I'm not sure. Ambulance, I think."

The calm voice asked for her postcode.

"Um, I don't have one. I'm on the moor somewhere near Furzewater Farm, but I can't see much because of the mist."

The calm voice asked for as much information as possible about Granfer's injuries and the location of Furzewater, and Katy agreed to try and get Granfer to the farm so he could be picked up. The voice said visibility might be too poor to send the air ambulance, but failing that an ambulance would come by road.

Katy plodded along the track she assumed would lead to Furzewater Farm, but the track became narrower and with alarm she realised she was lost. Muddy water had seeped in through the top of her short riding boots. Her socks were saturated and with every step she had stabbing pains from the raw blisters on her heels. She felt hot and sweaty, yet shivery at the same time. There was no point in turning back, but where was she going? Tears fell silently down her face as she trudged on.

She thought she heard a tractor somewhere, but her mind was probably playing tricks on her. She remembered how she'd imagined the noise of a tractor on the night she'd found Trifle as a newborn foal, tiny and trembling. "Now look at you!" she said, fondling the stocky pony walking by her side.

It really was a tractor! She was sure of it now. Trifle had heard it too. A grey shape loomed through the mist.

"Here! Over here!" Katy shouted, taking her hand off Granfer's leg and waving her arm. The tractor drove towards them. Bizarrely, it was followed by three silver jeeps. Katy wondered whether she was imagining things, especially when the tractor stopped beside her and a young man jumped down from the cab.

"Greg! What are you doing here?" she gasped.

"Our farm's got grazing rights up here. This film crew wanted some shots of moorland with livestock in the foreground, so I was trying to help out by feeding our animals where they wanted them, but unfortunately the mist's got the better of us," Greg replied. He looked at Granfer. "Is that Mr Squires? Is he all right?"

"G-G-Granfer's had a-an a-accident!" Katy stammered, and she burst into tears. Greg put his arms around her and gave her a hug. His jacket smelt of silage, but it was the best hug she'd ever had. "I-I'm lost, a-and the a-ambulance is going to F-Furzewater!" she sobbed.

"Well, we'd better get a move-on, then," said Greg.

He turned to the driver of the first jeep. "The man on this pony is cold and badly injured. Can you get him into your vehicle and drive him down to Furzewater Farm if I show you the way? Apparently an ambulance is going to pick him up from there. I'll ring the owners of the farm and warn them we're coming." Looking down at Katy again, he said, "Are you okay to ride after us?"

The film crew carried Granfer to the jeep. Then Greg lifted Katy onto Trifle and she followed the procession of vehicles down to Furzewater Farm, which was less than a mile away as it turned out. A girl in one of the jeeps had given Katy a chocolate bar, and she munched it as she rode along. Never before had chocolate tasted so good.

They arrived in the large farmyard of Furzewater Farm, and the Huxtables came rushing out with blankets and hot drinks. It was all rather unreal, Katy thought. Half an hour ago she'd felt as if she and Granfer were the only humans left on the planet. Now there were people everywhere.

There was a faint, deep, throbbing noise.

"The air ambulance! Here it comes!" one of the film crew shouted, pointing at a dark shape in the grey sky. Mr Huxtable hurried to the field behind the house where he'd marked out a landing site. Luckily, Trifle didn't seem to be worried by the huge, noisy monster in the sky. Perhaps she was too tired to notice.

The helicopter landed with pinpoint accuracy, and Granfer was soon flying off to hospital. Katy prayed she'd see him again.

10

The Turning Point

The film crew took Katy back to Barton Farm, followed by Greg towing Trifle in the Huxtables' livestock trailer.

As soon as he heard about the accident, Dad went to the hospital to be with his father. Greg offered to do the evening farm work and take care of the two ponies. Katy had a drink and a sandwich, and went to bed.

Mum made tea for the film crew, who were trying to control their excitement. They'd filmed a dramatic rescue which would feature on breakfast television news. Better still, they'd found Barton Farm – the ideal location for their new television series.

Katy was desperately tired, but she couldn't sleep. The events of the day kept playing on her mind, making her jittery. Had she been wrong to put Granfer on Trifle? Would it have been better to take Granfer to Barton? Did Greg think she was stupid, getting lost like that? Would Granfer be okay? Doubt and worry gnawed at her tired mind. She heard the film crew leave, and then Greg. Mum went outside to feed the dog and check on the ponies, and came in again. The telephone rang several times, and Mum recounted the same story in a tired voice. At last, there was a telephone call from Dad at the hospital.

"Phil! Thank goodness it's you! How's Jack? Oh, how marvellous! I'm so glad! Rachel's there with you? That's good. Greg's looked after the animals, and he's coming back to help tomorrow, bless him. Yes, poor Katy was exhausted; she fell asleep as soon as her head touched the pillow."

"I wish," Katy said to herself. She decided to go downstairs to find out about Granfer.

As she went downstairs she heard Mum say, "Phil, you know those people who brought Katy back home? Well, they're from the BBC and they think Barton will be the ideal setting for a children's television series. Also, one of the men saw your paintings in the sitting room, and he really liked them. I hope you don't mind, but he's taken some photos to show a friend who's an art dealer in London." She looked up and smiled at Katy as she walked into the kitchen. "Katy's just come down. Yes, I'll tell her. Oh, and watch breakfast TV – they said they'd run the story if everything turned out all right. I'd better ring them and let them know the good news. Lots of love. Bye, then."

Katy sat at the kitchen table. "How's Granfer?" she asked.

"He's okay," Mum said as she made them both some hot chocolate. "I mean, he'll have to stay in hospital for a while and his leg's badly damaged, but he's going to be all right."

"What's wrong with him?" Katy asked.

"Quite a lot of things: crushed leg, cracked ribs, shock and hypothermia, I think Dad said."

"Hypo-what?"

"Hypothermia. It's what happens when your body gets so cold it can't work properly. The doctor treating Granfer wants to meet you. He says you saved Granfer's life."

Katy blushed. "Rubbish! Trifle, Greg, the film crew, the air ambulance and the doctors saved his life." She'd been thinking a lot about the chain of events involved in Granfer's rescue. If one link had been removed, the outcome might have been very different.

*

The following day, the story featured on breakfast television. They even showed Katy leading Trifle over the moor, waving frantically, and there was a close-up of Granfer on Trifle.

"I didn't realise they were filming any of that!" Katy exclaimed when she saw it. She was incredibly grateful they hadn't included her blubbing while being hugged by Greg – if that had been on national television it would have been so embarrassing!

For a while Barton Farm was invaded by television reporters and journalists, and the telephone rang constantly. Katy had a taste of what it must be like to be a celebrity. At first it was good fun, but then it became rather annoying.

Fortunately it didn't carry on. Fresh events took over, and the uplifting story about a young girl and her Exmoor pony rescuing an old man from the middle of the moor became yesterday's news.

The film crew hadn't forgotten though. They returned to talk about using Barton Farm as the location for a television series. The amount of money offered for the deal was enough to pay off over half of Barton Farm's debt to the bank. The farm would be safe! The icing on the cake, as far as Katy was concerned, was that the series was to be called *Mousie* and it was based on Katy's favourite book of all time – a story about an Exmoor pony called *Moorland Mousie*. Granfer had given it to her on the day Trifle had been born, so it was special for all sorts of reasons.

Granfer's nerves in his left leg had been damaged so badly that he had to use a walking frame for a while. His dancing days were over, but at least he was alive.

Katy went to see him whenever she could. He was bored and frustrated by his lack of mobility. The news about the television crew and the possibility that there would be enough money to save the farm lifted his spirits tremendously though.

On one of her visits, Granfer showed Katy his photo albums with old pictures of the family and the farm. Everybody in the photos looked young, happy and carefree.

"We had the best of it, Katy," said Granfer. "Farming was fun in those days; there were plenty of people to lend a hand, and the shops wanted the food we produced."

Katy turned over a page of the album. An eye-catching painting of a Fordson Major tractor working in a field – unmistakably Broadacre at Barton Farm – slipped out onto the floor. Katy picked it up and looked at it. Stuck onto the back was a label which read, *Philip Squires. Winner of Southwest Young Artist Award, 14 years and under.* By the label, in her father's writing, Katy saw the words:

To Dad. Happy Birthday. Love, Phil

"Wow, Granfer! This is brilliant! Why didn't you get it framed?"

Granfer sighed. "Well, it was only a child's picture, and we didn't have money for that kind of thing. I didn't want to encourage Phil's liking for art too much. He had to farm Barton, not waste his time on a hobby with no future."

"No future! Haven't you heard, Granfer? Yesterday, a man from London came to Barton and bought some of Dad's paintings. He reckons they could sell for about £800 each!"

"People in London have more money than sense then," Granfer replied scornfully. "Why, you could buy a cow for that money!"

"Stop being grumpy, Granfer! The point is that Dad's paintings could just save the farm."

"Pah! The whole world's gone mad!" Granfer grumbled.

"Well, you could just be a bit happy for him!" Katy exclaimed, a deep sense of injustice consuming her. "I know Rachel's your favourite because she likes horses and all the things you like, but Dad's spent his whole life trying to please you! He nearly lost the farm, but that wasn't really his fault, and now his paintings could save it. Can't you see it would mean the world to him if you just praised him for once, rather than having a go at him all the time?" She held the picture out to Granfer. "I bet he was longing for you to frame this and put it up on your wall to show you were proud of him!" She instantly regretted what she'd said. She adored Granfer and she'd never spoken to him like that before.

He took the picture from Katy and sank back in his chair, looking weak and confused. "Perhaps you'd better go now, Katy," he said quietly.

Katy felt awful. She left, wishing she hadn't said anything.

11

Pure Gold

Following Katy's outburst, Granfer did a lot of thinking and he decided several things. One of those things was that he'd organise a party in the Town Hall for his golden wedding anniversary, as a surprise for Gran. He enlisted Melanie to help him organise everything. All the replies to the invitations were to be sent to Stonyford, to keep the party a secret. The local pub would arrange the bar and a buffet supper, and the same band which had played at Rachel's wedding would be hired.

All the guests were asked to arrive by a certain

time. Tom acted as a lookout, and as soon as he saw Gran and Granfer drive up to the Town Hall he rushed upstairs and shouted, "Quiet, everyone! They've arrived!"

The lights were turned out and everyone fell silent. Alice had come back from school especially for the party. She and Katy were sitting together, and they had to be silent for such a long time that they couldn't help giggling.

"Sshh!" Tom hissed.

The two friends grinned at each other. "I'm so glad you're here!" Katy whispered.

Before Tom could say "Sshh!" again, Gran and Granfer appeared in the doorway. The lights went on, and everyone jumped to their feet and yelled, "Happy Anniversary!"

Gran was overwhelmed. Several old friends had travelled miles to be there, and she went around the room greeting everyone with hugs, kisses and joyful exclamations.

Katy had so much to talk about with Alice that she was rather annoyed when the tables were cleared away and the band started to play. They partnered each other for the first few dances, and then a boy who was two years above Katy at school asked Alice to dance. Katy was without a dancing partner, so she went to sit with Gran and Granfer.

"Having a good time, Katy?" asked Granfer.

"Yes thanks, Granfer." Katy glanced rather enviously at Alice, who was obviously enjoying herself. She looked around to see if Rachel and Mark were there. "Where's Rachel?"

"I expect she'll be here soon," Granfer replied. He didn't seem particularly worried that Rachel was missing the party. How odd.

The caller announced The West Country Waltz, and Alice's partner wasted no time in claiming her. It looks as if I won't be dancing again this evening, Katy thought glumly.

"Excuse me, may I have the pleasure of this dance?"

Greg! Katy's spirits soared.

"I hope you can remember how to do this, because I haven't got a clue!" Greg smiled at Katy as he put his arm around her.

She went weak at the knees and wondered whether she'd be able to move at all. To begin with, they got into a terrible muddle and couldn't stop laughing, but by the end of the dance they were doing pretty well.

To Katy's delight, Greg stayed with her for the next couple of dances. Then the band stopped playing, a huge cake was produced and Gran and Granfer were helped onto the stage. The cake was cut, and everyone gave three cheers. Granfer raised his hand and the guests fell silent. Katy noticed he was trembling.

"Peggy and I are very grateful to you all for turning up this evening. It means a lot to us," he started in a shaky voice. "I'm not very good at expressing my feelings, but tonight I feel that I ought to. Jack Squires isn't going soft in the head; he's going to say a few things which should have been said years ago.

"First, I love you, Peggy. You're the best wife any man could wish for, and I'm very lucky you've put up with me for so long. I'd like you all to raise your glasses to Peggy, my golden girl!"

"To Peggy!" everyone repeated as they drank a toast to her.

Gran wiped her eyes with a tissue, and smiled.

"Next, I would like to say how proud I am of our son, Phil. He's been through some difficult times, many of them caused by me, but he's come through triumphant. I'm such a pig-headed old fool that I couldn't see what a gifted artist he was. I made him farm Barton when he wanted to study art. Now, it seems that his paintings are earning more than a pen of fat lambs! Well, Phil, at least I can say that I'm the proud owner of one of your earlier works!" Granfer held a framed picture above his head for the party guests to see. It was the prize-winning picture Phil had given to his father.

Katy's parents were standing nearby, and she heard her dad saying, "I thought he'd thrown that away ages ago!"

"I treasure this, son. Thank you. I can't tell you how proud I am," Granfer said.

Everyone started clapping and cheering. Dad beamed. Mum put her arm around him and hugged him.

"Now then, where was I? This emotional stuff can put a man off his stride, you know," Granfer said. "Oh, yes! Where's Katy? There you are! Come on up here!"

Katy blushed and shook her head, but Greg pushed her towards the stage. She climbed the stairs, and looked down at a sea of faces smiling up at her. Granfer put his arm around her shoulders. There was a commotion at the back of the hall, and several people started talking excitedly. She couldn't see what was going on.

"Our granddaughter, Katy, is a very special girl," Granfer continued, unperturbed. "She's made me see what's important in life. It isn't where you live or what you do or whether you win prizes in competitions. Love, family and friendships are the things that are important. I am lucky enough to have been blessed with all these things, thanks to all of you here tonight."

There was another round of applause, and then someone walked through the crowd of guests, followed by a camera crew. Everyone gasped in astonishment. As the man came nearer, Katy recognised him as her favourite TV presenter, Steve Harding. He presented *Pure Gold Pets*.

Steve Harding walked up the steps and onto the stage, the camera crew following his every move. Katy started to walk away to the other side of the stage. They must have come to film Granfer because of his Exmoor ponies, and she'd be in the way.

"Katy Squires! Where are you off to, young lady? We've come to talk to you about your Pure Gold Pet, Trifle, the Exmoor pony," Steve Harding said. His voice sounded very loud because he was wearing a microphone.

The guests began to clap, and Katy nearly fainted. She stared at the lights above the camera like a startled rabbit.

Steve Harding was used to filling in awkward silences from people who were star-struck. He turned to face the cameras. "On a cold, misty February morning ..." Steve recounted the story of Granfer's rescue, spiced with a bit of dramatic exaggeration here and there. " ... And that's how Katy Squires and her faithful friend, Trifle, saved the life of Jack Squires," he concluded the tale of Granfer's rescue. "However, the story does not end there. I understand that Katy's family farm was going to have to be sold. Trifle's heroic rescue was reported on television and, as a result, a major film contract for the TV series *Mousie* has been signed. And that's not all; Katy's father, Phillip Squires, has at last received the recognition he deserves for his superb paintings. So, one brave little pony has saved a life and a family farm business, as well as revealing a great artistic talent. If you'll follow me downstairs, ladies and gentlemen, we'll go and join the heroine herself. She can do many things but, unfortunately, walking upstairs isn't one of them!"

Trifle was standing in a blaze of lights in the entrance to the Town Hall. Rachel was holding her. Trifle looked remarkably calm. In fact, she looked as if she was thoroughly enjoying herself.

"Did you know about this?" Katy whispered to Granfer.

"Afraid so," Granfer confessed, grinning. "You've got Alice to thank for it, though. She was the one who nominated Trifle for the award. It's a proper friend you've got there."

"I know," Katy agreed. "Alice is the best!"

Trifle didn't even mind when champagne corks started popping. With Rachel and Katy by her side, she wasn't afraid of anything. Glasses full of champagne were passed around, and then Steve Harding presented

Trifle with a Pure Gold Pet medal, which hung round her neck on a wide blue and gold ribbon.

"A bit more becoming than a stirrup leather wrapped in a coat!" Granfer said to Katy with a wink.

"Ladies and gentlemen!" Steve Harding announced grandly. "Please raise your glasses and drink a toast to Trifle, the champion pony!"

"Trifle, the champion pony!"

Katy's Pony Surprise, the third book in the trilogy, is available from June.
Here is a preview of the first chapter.

1

New Neighbours

As Katy rode her Exmoor pony, Trifle, along the lane from Barton Farm, she felt she was the luckiest girl in the world. Although it was odd to think about Christmas on the first day of the summer holidays, Katy decided she felt the same sort of excitement as on Christmas morning when there was a stocking full of presents at the end of her bed. Also, she thought, holidays are like Christmas stockings because most things are half-expected but there are always some complete surprises tucked in between. For instance, this summer she knew there'd be horse shows, Pony Club camp, picnics, long rides, lazy days and having fun with her best friend, Alice. But the surprises – well, if she knew what they were going to be, they wouldn't be surprises.

"Next week it's Pony Club camp, Trifle. I'm afraid you'll have to go because poor old Jacko's still lame from that horrid nail he trod on last winter. Anyway, it'll do you good to have a bit of proper schooling. You'll learn how to jump too; that'll be fun!" Katy leaned forward and pretended to ride like a jockey. Trifle felt the shift in her weight and accelerated into a canter. Laughing at the eagerness of her pony, Katy sat up straight again and closed her fingers gently on the reins. Trifle eased back into a steady trot.

They rounded a sharp bend and skidded to a halt. Katy bumped her nose on Trifle's neck, and just managed to save herself from falling off by grabbing a handful of bushy mane.

The lane was blocked by a huge removal lorry. A couple of men in blue overalls, supervised by a dark-haired man wearing a black leather jacket and blue jeans, were using a very noisy electric ramp to unload furniture.

"Oh!" Katy exclaimed. "Wellsworthy Farm must have been sold. That was quick! We can't get past the lorry, so I suppose we'll have to turn back."

"Hi, there!" the man in the leather jacket shouted, raising his hand in greeting. "Hang on a minute!"

Katy tried her best to hang on a minute; Trifle was dancing on the spot with agitation. The man's eyes were hidden by expensive-looking sunglasses but, as he came closer, Katy could see a smile on his lined, suntanned face. He gave Trifle a hearty pat on the neck, which was more like hitting than patting, and she tried to shy away.

"Nice little Shetland pony you've got there," the man said, nimbly avoiding Trifle's hooves as they tap-danced on the tarmac. "I've just bought this place. Who are you? I'm Dean, by the way."

Katy was just about to speak when Dean gave Trifle another slap and asked, "What's his name?"

Trifle spun round, pushing him to one side.

"Oops! Sorry!" Katy said. "I'm Katy Squires, and I live at Barton Farm, about a mile up that lane. This is my Exmoor pony, Trifle. She's only four, so she gets a bit nervous about new things like removal lorries. And she's a mare – a girl, not a boy."

"Exmoor, Shetland, mare, stallion – they're all the same to me, I'm afraid. Dangerous at both ends and uncomfortable in the middle. Hang about! You're the girl who was on the telly with a pony who saved somebody's life! Is that the pony?" Dean gave Trifle another hit-pat, and she decided she'd had enough.

"Yes, she rescued Granfer – my grandfather. Sorry! Got to go! Nice to meet you!" Katy said quickly, as Trifle set off down the lane, cantering sideways.

"I like the circus trick!" Dean called out. "What do you do for an encore?"

Katy barely heard him above the noise of Trifle's clattering hooves as she flew round the corner, heading for the safety of home.

*

Katy's mum was in the kitchen at Barton Farm, talking on the telephone. She broke off from her conversation as Katy appeared. "Boots off! And what are you doing with that bucket?"

"Um, I just need a bucket of warm water from the sink so I can wash Trifle," Katy replied. "She's all sweaty."

Mum sighed. "Go on then, but don't spill any." Her attention returned to the telephone. "Sorry, Melanie. Where was I? Yes, the new kitchen's wonderful, but I don't know how long I'll manage to keep it that way," she said, watching as Katy struggled to squeeze the bucket under the elegant mixer tap of the new sink.

"Oh, are you talking to Alice's mum?" Katy asked.

"Yes, attempting to."

"Can you ask if it's okay for me to go over to Stonyford this afternoon? Alice and I want to get everything sorted for camp."

"Melanie heard you, and she says that's fine. She'll give you a lesson on Trifle if you get there by two-thirty. We're having salad for lunch as it's such a hot day, so you can have it early if you like."

"Ideal! Thanks!" Katy said, sloshing water onto the floor as she carried the heavy, steaming bucket to the door. "Oops, sorry!" she called over her shoulder.

Katy turned Trifle out in the field with Jacko after

she'd been washed, so her coat would dry in the sunshine. She watched while her ponies greeted each other like long-lost friends. Then Trifle wandered away, pawed the ground, circled, crumpled, rolled, sat up for a moment and clambered to her feet again, shaking herself and snorting with satisfaction before settling down to the serious business of eating as much grass as possible.

Even now, Katy found it hard to believe she actually owned the two ponies. She'd bought Trifle as a newly weaned foal from Brendon pony sale, and had kept her in secret at Stonyford for her first winter. During that time, Melanie had taught her to ride on Jacko, a handsome liver chestnut gelding Katy had loved from the start. Granfer had found out about Trifle while he was arranging to buy Jacko for Katy as a present, and on her birthday she'd had the biggest surprise of her life when both Jacko and Trifle had arrived at Barton Farm. Over three years had passed since that day, but she still remembered every detail. She smiled to herself as she watched Jacko and Trifle grazing side by side.

Katy sometimes wondered what her life would be like if Alice hadn't moved to Stonyford with her mum and twin brothers. She probably wouldn't own Trifle, certainly wouldn't own Jacko and she wouldn't have a best friend – not like Alice, anyway. Also, if she really thought about it, Barton Farm would have been sold by now, her family would be miserable and Mum most definitely wouldn't have a brand new kitchen, paid for with the income from Dad's paintings. In fact, Granfer could be… Yes, it was scary thinking about what life would be like if the Gardners hadn't moved into Stonyford.

"Lunch time!" Mum called.

"Coming!" Katy replied, and after one last look at the ponies she hurried indoors.

"I thought you said you were just going for a gentle hack this morning. How come Trifle got so sweaty?" Mum asked as she sliced a home-made loaf fresh from the Aga.

The smell of the bread made Katy realise how hungry she was. "I meant to go for a gentle hack, but Trifle had other ideas. It wasn't her fault, though – not really. You see, we met the man who's bought Wellsworthy. He was there with a removal lorry, and he came up to say hello."

"Really? What's he like?"

"Well, Trifle didn't think much of him. He wears those odd sunglasses which look like mirrors, and he obviously doesn't know the first thing about horses – he's one of those people who thinks the right way to greet a horse is to slap it. Oh, and he's called Dean."

Mum looked amused. "Poor Dean! It appears

he's managed to fall out with his most important neighbour, an Exmoor pony, before he's even set foot in his new home!"

Trifle looked very surprised and rather grumpy when Katy caught her, tacked her up and set off on another ride after lunch. However, she soon perked up, especially when she realised where they were going. She seemed to love Stonyford almost as much as Katy did.

They took the field and moorland route, avoiding the Wellsworthy lane. Riding through the fields meant going through several gates, but Katy didn't mind because she was trying to teach Trifle how to open them.

It's amazing how quickly Trifle learns new things once she understands what she's supposed to do, Katy thought as Trifle headed for the correct end of the gate onto the Common, and stood with her head over it and her body close to the post so Katy could undo the latch. "Push it," she said, and Trifle pushed the gate open with her chest, walked through on command, turned in a tight circle and stood still on the other side while Katy did up the latch again. "Good girl!" she said, stroking Trifle's neck. "What a clever pony you are."

They had plenty of time, thanks to an early lunch,

so Katy had decided they should walk most of the way to save Trifle's energy for their lesson with Melanie. However, Trifle jigged around so much once they were on the Common that Katy couldn't resist letting her gallop some of the way.

"Yippee! Hurray for the holidays!" Katy shouted as Trifle raced over the heather.

Despite their gallop, the journey seemed to take longer than usual, probably because Katy couldn't wait to see Alice again. They'd remained best friends even though they now went to different schools; Katy went to the local secondary school and Alice went to a boarding school miles away. This made the holidays even more special, and they spent as much time as possible with each other. There was so much Katy wanted to tell Alice, including the news about Wellsworthy.

At last they reached the back entrance to Stonyford, and Trifle announce their arrival with an excited whinny. Katy giggled; it was like sitting on a mini-earthquake when Trifle whinnied.

Alice ran to the gate, opened it and bowed with a flourish. "Behold! Trifle the Wonder Horse!" she announced with extreme grandness. "Are you too famous to grace our humble home now you're a TV celebrity? We'll have to feed you chocolate-coated apples and put champagne in your water buckets."

"She's fizzy enough as it is, thanks," Katy said. "I had a job to stop her on the Common just now."

"Why, hello!" said Alice in mock surprise. "I didn't see you up there!"

"Well, I'd better come down to your level then," Katy replied. She made a clicking sound with her tongue, and Trifle instantly dropped her head to the ground so Katy could slide down her neck. "Tra-lah! That's our latest trick."

"Trifle! Is there no end to your talents?" Alice asked.

The girls laughed. Little did they know they'd soon find out.

Author's Note

This story is set on Exmoor, a beautiful National Park in the south west of England. It's a place very close to my heart because I'm lucky enough to live on a farm on Exmoor. Although Barton Farm is fictional, it has a lot of things in common with our farm, with its Red Ruby Devon cattle, Exmoor Horn sheep and a herd of free-living Exmoor ponies. Stonyford is also fictional, but the villages in this story really do exist and the long-distance ride described in this book follows actual rights of way.

*

All the human and equine characters in this series are fictional, but many people and ponies I've known throughout my life have given me inspiration in one way or another. For example, Katy was the name of my best friend at my first school, and a wonderful neighbouring farmer who was a great countryman was called Granfer by his family.

Of the ponies which have helped me with this book, a Welsh cob called Jacko and two Exmoor ponies called Mike and Tinkerbell have been particularly important.

Jacko was my first pony, and to me he was the best pony in the world. Like the Jacko in this story, he was a handsome liver chestnut gelding who was safe, reliable and fun. We went on several long rides together, including a trek along the South Downs Way and some rides over Exmoor.

Mike belonged to a neighbour called Ken Walker, who bought him from Bampton Fair as a newly weaned foal. When Mike was four years old, my husband Chris trained him to be ridden. Although Mike was nervous he was a quick learner, and after a while we were going on long rides over the moor with him. Ken was so delighted with our progress that he entered Mike for a ridden class at Exford Show. Well, the excitement was too much for Mike, and I'm afraid he behaved rather like Trifle did at Exford Show in this story – except he bucked Chris off in front of the judge!

Tinkerbell is slow and arthritic now, but she used to be a bundle of energy. She was our daughter Sarah's pony when they were both much younger, and she taught her many things – including how to stay on, no matter what! Both she and Sarah gave me lots of ideas for these stories about Katy and Trifle. For instance, Tinks loved to travel and was always eager to be loaded into any lorry or trailer for a ride, so we often used her as a companion for horses and ponies which were frightened of travelling.

Our herd of free-living Exmoor ponies, which we keep on the moorland above our farm, have also provided me with a great deal of inspiration. Over the years I've handled several of them as weaned foals, wild off the moor. I've learned a great deal from the ponies themselves, and also from a natural horsewoman called Vanessa Bee and her husband Philip.

The story about Moon being stolen in this book may seem far-fetched, but something similar happened to some friends of mine. They lent their mare to another family, and a couple of years later they were told the pony had died. In fact, she'd been sold for a lot of money; they discovered this when she was spotted at a horse show, alive and well.

*

It's hard to mention individual people for fear of leaving someone out, but friends who have given me particular help and encouragement are Marcia Monbleau, Sally Chapman-Walker, Sue Baker and Sue Croft and, of course, my Mum.

Most of all, thanks and love to Chris, my very patient and understanding husband, and our children, George and Sarah. Chris has supported me in countless ways, including providing illustrations for this book. He also gave me the idea for Granfer's accident, as he fell off his quad bike when he was counting deer for the annual survey. I'm afraid I didn't rescue him with an Exmoor pony, though!

Last, but not least, many thanks to Fiona Kennedy, Felicity Johnston and the team at Orion for all their invaluable guidance and hard work.

Exmoor Ponies

Exmoor ponies, or "Exmoors" as they are often called, are a very special breed. They are the only native pony breed that has the same characteristics as the original British Hill Pony that came to the British Isles about one hundred and thirty thousand years ago. Various studies of the bones, teeth and genetics of Exmoor ponies have supported this.

Why Exmoor ponies have survived as nature intended, whereas other breeds have been altered by man, is a bit of a mystery. Historically, Exmoor was a wild, sparsely populated area, which was reserved as a Royal Forest or hunting ground. There were no significant trade routes through the area, and no important towns nearby. It seems that, because of this, Exmoor had little contact with the rest of Britain and the wild ponies within the Forest remained an isolated, pure population.

In 1818, the Forest was sold to an industrialist

called John Knight. Several local farmers bought some of the wild ponies and started up herds of their own, including the former warden of Exmoor Forest, Sir Thomas Acland. He founded the Acland herd, now the Anchor herd, which can be seen on Winsford Hill.

The Exmoor Pony Society was founded in 1921, with the purpose of keeping the breed true to type.

During the Second World War, many ponies were stolen for food and fewer ponies were bred. In the end, only about forty-six mares and four stallions were left on Exmoor. A remarkable lady called Mary Etherington encouraged some Exmoor farmers to re-establish their herds so that the breed was saved. However, it is still classified as endangered by the Rare Breeds Survival Trust.

Exmoor ponies make history come to life. It is up to all of us to ensure they have a future.

If you'd like to find out more about Exmoor ponies, the Exmoor Pony Society has a very good website www.exmoorponysociety.org.uk with lots of information and details of ponies for sale or loan. The secretary is called Sue McGeever, and her telephone number is (01884) 839930.

A visit to Exmoor isn't complete without a trip to the Exmoor Pony Centre, near Dulverton. This is the headquarters of the Moorland Mousie Trust, a charity dedicated to the welfare and promotion of Exmoor ponies. Admission to see the ponies and their pony-themed gift shop is free, but you can also book pony handling sessions for beginners or rides on the moor for experienced riders. For details see the website www.exmoorponycentre.org.uk or telephone (01398) 323093. The Trust runs a pony adoption scheme – the next best thing to owning an Exmoor pony!

Want the chance to adopt a pony

at the EXMOOR PONY CENTRE for one year?

Adopt an EXMOOR PONY!

ALL YOU HAVE TO DO TO ENTER IS EMAIL:
competitions@orionbooks.co.uk
with the subject heading "Exmoor Pony" and
one lucky winner will win a year's pony sponsorship.

The closing date for the competition is 1st September 2012. For full terms and conditions visit the Orion website:
www.orionbooks.co.uk/terms-and-conditions